The
GREAT HIVE

To Jack,

Hope you enjoy!

Joseph Pellegrino

A Real Hero

Tate Publishing & *Enterprises*

The Great Hive

Published by Tate Publishing & Enterprises, LLC
127 E. Trade Center Terrace | Mustang, Oklahoma 73064 USA
1.888.361.9473 | www.tatepublishing.com

Tate Publishing is committed to excellence in the publishing industry. The company reflects the philosophy established by the founders, based on Psalm 68:11,
"The Lord gave the word and great was the company of those who published it."

Cover design by Cole Roberts
Interior design by Nathan Harmony

Published in the United States of America

ISBN: 978-1-61566-151-0
1. Fiction: Action & Adventure
2. Fiction: Coming of Age
09.10.07

This book is dedicated to my parents, who gave me the necessary support and love when I needed it the most as I chronicled Anthony's first adventure. I know that they will be there for me as I continue my own personal adventure as an author, which is only just beginning.

Part One: Beginning Anew

Prologue

An ominous buzzing echoed through the Hive of Vesthrax as mourners assembled to bury their deceased monarch, Queen Vespa the First. Thousands of hornets and wasps gathered to pay their last respects to the honorable ruler. The crowd's buzzing died down as the high priest hovered over the grave. "Loyal Subjects of the Hive," he began in a voice withered with age, "we have gathered here today to honor the late Queen Vespa. After years of prosperity, her reign has at last come to a noble conclusion. However, as tradition dictates, it is with a heavy heart that I deem Princess Iriana queen of the Hive of Vesthrax."

With that a chorus of cheers rose from the crowd. Princess Iriana flared her wings proudly as the high priest set the beautifully carved mother-of-pearl tiara upon her head. As the slightly less dismal crowd receded, Iriana

waited in a silent crouch. To any curious passerby it would seem that she was mourning the loss of her mother. However, she most certainly wasn't. In fact, that was the exact opposite of what she was doing. Iriana chuckled, then started giggling wildly. Eventually it became a spine-chilling belly laugh.

An insect laugh is an odd noise that varies according to the type of humor. The laugh of a wasp or hornet is an ugly sound, the sound of water sputtering from a sprinkler head perturbed by a stubborn layer of mud. This isn't because they are ugly creatures by nature, although this one was.

"Finally, *Queen* Iriana; that has a nice ring to it," she whispered to herself. Iriana made a check on her mental to-do list.

"Would it really have hurt to wait for her to die of natural causes?" Her gaze was diverted to the domed stained-glass ceiling and the imposing figure descending from the observation balcony.

"Of course not, General," she stated simply. "But then again, what would be the fun in that?" The general grinned malevolently, concealing his partial unease at the statement, his eyes shining beneath the beams of moonlight.

"When shall I begin the army's proceedings?" the general asked. Iriana shook her head.

"Patience, patience, General, all in due time. You can't build an empire in one day."

Don't talk to me *about patience,* the general thought bitterly. *You poisoned your own mother because you couldn't wait one more month for the old crone to start pushing up daisies.*

But like always, he nodded his agreement obediently. He paused in thought.

"Your Highness," he asked, "hasn't the operation already begun?" Iriana glanced around suspiciously.

"You should be more wary of your tongue, General. We wouldn't want the wrong creatures to hear you." Iriana disappeared into the darkest nearby hallway, the general retired to his quarters, and the great domed cathedral was left in silence. By then the entire kingdom was asleep, with only two key figures aware of the sinister plot about to unfold. Thus began the rise of Iriana the Terrible.

Preparation

Thrust, withdraw, fling, thrust, withdraw, fling, Anthony Daemond repeated mentally. That was his memorized routine as he gouged open the rock walls of the colony's mines. It was nearly time for the colony's triennial Moon Festival, a ceremony of jubilation, merriment, feasting, and drinking, renowned throughout the land.

For the last ten days Anthony and his fellow worker ants had been mining the precious moonstones required for the festival. In fact, they were currently surrounded by the clear glass stones that were lodged in the rock walls. As the bell sounded for lunch, Anthony tossed his pickaxe aside and whistled to Artie, his pet aphid.

Anthony and Artie had been thick as thieves since they were both larvae. Even with Artie's company, Anthony often felt as if he were alone in the world ever since his father, Cyrus Daemond, had been arrested for protesting against longer work shifts. Immediately after being released on parole, he left the colony under mysterious circumstances and was not seen or heard from again. From that point on, it had all been downhill for Anthony and his mother, and he had taken it upon himself to fill his father's working position. Anthony Daemond belonged to the species *Camponotus ferrugineus,* the red carpenter ant. He was one inch long and a bright shade of crimson brown. He was a teenaged ant and would soon be a young ant. When that time came, Anthony would finally grow his wings. Having wings was every young male ant's dream, soon to be his reality. Celia Astaire, acknowledging the symptoms of one of her friend's sulking spells, rushed over to comfort him.

"I don't understand why you feel the need to dwell on the past. Try to look on the bright side of things. At least you aren't stuck picking leaves off of trees," Celia pointed out, gesturing toward a group of harvester ants. Anthony thought she made a good point, but he was too annoyed by her know-it-all attitude to admit it.

"You know what," Celia said, "maybe you should find a girlfriend." Anthony choked on his drink.

"Celia, I am surrounded by girls all day long, and most of them are my bosses. All they ever do is nitpick at every insignificant detail and get on my case about... well, everything. So why would I want any of them in my personal life?"

"I'm just saying, since your dad left, you've been sort of depressed, and everybody has noticed," Celia explained.

"Depressed? I'm not depressed! How long has every-

one been talking about this behind my back?" Anthony asked, startled.

"Just about ... forever, actually. If you weren't so isolated, you would know that," Celia said.

"This conversation is getting me depressed," Anthony said. "So let's switch to a lighter topic. Do you have anything special planned for the Moon Festival this year?"

"Well, I wanted it to be a surprise, but since you asked, I guess I'll show you. Just don't go flapping your gums about it, okay? This is going to be special." Celia led Anthony away from the work area to her apartment cell and showed him into a large art room with decorative stones, a sculptor's tools, canvases, and other art appliances. In the center of the room was some sculpture hidden by a dusty brown tarp.

"This is my greatest work—a masterpiece constructed by weeks of sweat, tears, and the raw determination to bring home the Gold Craft Medal," Celia announced proudly. She pulled the tarp away dramatically.

"Whoa," Anthony gasped in awe. Before him was a beautifully detailed alabaster statue of Agoz the ant god, decorated with moonstones. Agoz was depicted as a large, powerful-looking ant with black armor, which Celia sculpted with coal. A real linen cape was sewn through the armored shoulder plates, and the statue's left hand rested on a sword of onyx. "Celia, why, this is amazing! How could you possibly *not* win?"

"Thanks!" said Celia. "I planned on a gold finish, but I couldn't afford it. I had to sell a lot of paintings for these materials Sadly, what little money I had originally saved for this project had to be spent on more practical items," she said, indicating the meager cache of assorted foods wedged into the floor of the apartment. Celia made money off of her paintings, and Anthony worked in tunnels and mines for low wages, making just enough to keep him and his mother fed. It wasn't great, but it was home. Every night when Anthony rested, he would think to himself, *When I'm old enough, I'll help the colony and everyone who lives in it, whatever it takes.*

"Now, what do *you* plan on doing for the festival?" Celia questioned Anthony.

Before he could reply, Anthony's attention was drawn to the balcony by an earsplitting bellow.

Rescue

"Anthony, where are you going?" Without a second thought, Anthony swung off of the balcony railing and dashed to the source of the roar, dodging past the crowds of terrified ants. Lumbering through the bottom-level entryway was a colossal beast at least three feet in length with an elongated, almost worm-like snout and claws like spear tips. On its back were the mangiest-looking ants Anthony had ever seen, some with eye-patches, and others with bolas and nooses. They were slavemaker ants. Some were mercenaries from army ant colonies. They emerged from a platform-like structure fastened to the creature's back with an array of straps.

All around him ants were being bound in thick ropes of twine and hauled onto the creature's back. Anthony looked around for the guards just in time to witness the guards being lapped up by the beast's writhing tongue. A burly looking ant toppled Anthony with a swift fling of a boomerang. Another pair of slavemakers bound his forelegs.

"Anthony, get over here and save me!"

Anthony whipped around to answer Celia's desperate cry but could not trace her voice to the location. Silently, he crawled on six legs to a tool bench while his captor wasn't looking, took up his pickax after sawing off the rope that bound his wrists, and then recklessly swung it at the nearest slaver. Anthony was unaccustomed to fighting unless it was with his friends in the clay beds, so he wasn't exactly sure whether he felt satisfaction or revulsion when the pickaxe decapitated the slaver with a sickening crunch.

When the other slavemakers saw this, fifteen others began closing in on him, jabbing at him with iron spear tips and blades. Anthony held the pickaxe feebly in front of him, uncomfortably aware of how pathetic he probably looked. One joined Anthony in the ring, his spear raised above his head. The slavemaker ants hissed and jeered at Anthony from their circle.

"Take his head off!" one cried.

"Gut him, Eliye!" shouted another.

"Chop the little runt to pieces!" others joined in. Anthony danced away as the ant named Eliye thrust the spear toward him. The cut rope that was used to tie up Anthony still lay on the ground next to the tool bench, which he grabbed and used like a whip. Eliye again lashed out with his spear like greased lightning, and again Anthony dodged. On the third attack he jumped over the slaver's jab and brought his feet down on the spear's

wooden shaft, snapping the steel head off. Anthony then knocked the broken pole out of Eliye's hand and wrapped the rope around his throat till he collapsed, unconscious.

The ring of slavemaker ants broke as Anthony heard a slow thumping coming toward him, and some of them muttered evilly. "Balg's gonna eat this one alive," one whispered eagerly. Anthony could only stare in horror at what was the biggest, scariest ant he had ever seen. He had heard stories of the army ants of the south (particularly South America), but they were much more frightening in person.

The army ant, Balg, was somewhere over two inches in length, which is an oddity because army ants are usually just over one inch, and was covered in plated lamellar armor. His helmet was fashioned from the head of a rhinoceros beetle, complete with the horn. Balg's scythe-shaped mandibles parted in a tremendous roar. Slowly, he lumbered toward Anthony with a mace raised in his left hand. Anthony bolted away as Balg brought the spiked head down with tremendous force, smashing a wooden bench.

Anthony quickly climbed over a small gate, the towering army ant smashing through it just a moment after he got over. Anthony dashed through the food court pit for the far side of the building. Balg was in hot pursuit, gaining on him with surprising speed. As Anthony reached the vendors at the far end, his pursuer halted six inches away from him. Balg hefted a table onto his shoulders, lifted it above his head, and threw it at Anthony. Fortunately enough, it missed Anthony. But the next table almost didn't. The picnic table was an even closer call. It was a

cycle: Balg threw, Anthony dodged. It seemed as though he would never run out of tables.

Balg reached into the kitchen and pulled out a metal cauldron, swinging it by the handle. He tossed it high over Anthony's head, and it collided with a loud crash against the wooden beams supporting the ceiling. Splinters of wood and chunks of rubble tumbled to the ground, and debris was flung in every direction. Anthony shielded himself underneath a niche in the wall as rock crashed down around him. As he crawled out of his hiding spot, Balg climbed over the debris, the morning star once again raised over his head. From the ceiling, another loose beam fell, not killing Anthony but pinning him to the ground. He waited for the impending strike, but it never came.

Instead, Balg howled in pain and lowered his weapon. Standing behind Balg was Celia, who had struck his leg with a lit torch. Seeing his chance to escape, Anthony lifted the beam. Anthony couldn't help but admire his puberty-imbued strength before pivoting around with the beam, knocking Balg to the ground.

"Where have you been?" Anthony asked Celia.

"I've been busy," she answered. "What have you been doing?"

"I've been fighting a giant army ant," Anthony answered. "Thanks, by the way." But then a miraculous humming was heard from above the ceiling. A multitude of insects garbed in red and yellow flew through the hole in the ceiling and descended upon the scores of slavemakers and mercenaries. An intense, if brief, battle ensued.

All of the slavemakers were killed, brutally injured, or

retreated. An enormously muscular goliath beetle bearing a deadly double-headed battleaxe frightened the anteater beast back out through the crumbled east side of the colony. Before Balg could strike again, *thwack, thwack*, the beetle dispatched him with two swings of his axe. Anthony had never been so awe-inspired in all his life. He meekly approached the obvious leader of the group, a horsefly. "Who are you, sir?" Anthony asked breathlessly.

"What business is it of yours?" the horsefly snapped in response.

"It was just a harmless question," said Celia.

"Normally I don't waste my time with annoying larvae, but if you must know, I'm Hawthorne, an Insect Champion of the Great Hive. Our sole duty is to maintain peace in the insect world and vanquish those who aim toward evil goals."

"That sounded rehearsed," said Celia.

"It was."

Anthony had a sudden flashback.

Before his father's arrest, Anthony's mother told him stories about a remarkable place called the Great Hive, where insects of all different species coexisted in harmony and studied the ways of the world. It was home to a select group of insects called the Insect Champions, who dedicated their lives to thwarting injustice. The beauty of the legendary place had haunted his daydreams ever since.

"How can I become a Champion?" Hawthorne was totally taken aback by Anthony's question.

"Quite frankly, you can't. You would have to travel there on foot, and we don't just accept *anyone* into our ranks, you

know. What you *can* do is go back home before you get killed!" As Hawthorne stormed off, the fierce-looking goliath beetle approached Anthony with a warm expression.

"Don't let Hawthorne's words discourage you," he said, throwing a frosty glare at Hawthorne. His voice carried a thick African accent. "An eager lad like you is just what the Hive needs. My name is Gregorak—you can call me Greg—and I believe you have the potential that Hawthorne fails to acknowledge. Don't tell him I said this, but sometimes he can be a real jerk. But as he warned, a journey to the Great Hive on foot is not one to be taken lightly. Unwary travelers don't have a chance of braving the treacherous terrain that overshadows the path. It's bad enough traveling in these parts with the wolf spiders roaming everywhere, but unless you can find a detour around the swamp, one has very little chance of surviving the trip."

I've been waiting for this opportunity my entire life. I can handle any obstacle in my path as long as that path leads to a great future, Anthony thought. "I'm ready," Anthony answered.

"Anthony, wait!" Celia called. "I'm coming with you!"

"Celia, are you sure ..." Anthony trailed off.

"Of course I'm coming. You weren't considering leaving without me, were you?"

"Of course not," Anthony replied sarcastically. "After all, how would I *ever* be able to make the trip without you?" Before they could set off, Gregorak pulled them back by the scruffs of their necks.

"You don't expect to make the trip without the needed provisions, do you? Go pack, and then you may take your leave."

Somewhere far in the distance, a mantis was conjuring a mental connection with a young ant.

"Yes," he whispered, "this knave is destined for greatness, and with his assistance, we shall guide our precious civilization through the great troubles that are nearing."

"Are you sure this is the one?" another voice asked.

"Yes, this time I am positive."

A Legacy and a Gift

At Anthony's household, his mother, Darcy, was preparing a dinner of boiled cabbage with almond sprinkles and a side dish of peach meringue. Anthony tiptoed silently toward his room, but Artie came rushing through the doorway, barking in his odd chirpish tone. When Darcy spotted her son, she treated him to one of her best, if not humiliating, bear hugs.

"Oh, Annie, I was so worried about you. Are you hurt? Where's—"

"Mom, please," Anthony cut in. "I'm fine!" He cautiously tried to pack his duffel bag. He *almost* had everything, but his mom asked the dreaded question: "Where are you going, sweetie?" Anthony had desperately wished to avoid the question, but it was too late now. So he took it step by step, explaining how he and Celia had been res-

cued, how the Champions' arrival connected to everything he'd been imagining, and how he'd known that there had always been something more to his miserable life.

When Anthony finished, he was expecting his mother to plead him to stay, but instead he received something totally different. A warm smile spread across Mrs. Daemond's face as tears of amazement welled up in her eyes.

"I knew they'd find their way here someday," she said. "I knew you would find that you didn't belong here. Your father said that you would sense your destiny, Anthony, and reach out for it." Mrs. Daemond collected herself for a moment. "Sit down, and I'll explain."

"Your father and I met just after I became a mother of one, instead of queen of a colony. We were both so eager to mate that we married immediately. Unfortunately, I never found out about his occupation as an IC (Insect Champion) until he returned home with a missing limb." She sighed longingly as she dwelled in forgotten memories. Anthony remembered how his father had to walk with a limp because had only six limbs. Before she could continue, Anthony leapt up from his chair.

"Why did you hide this from me?" he asked angrily. "If you had told me earlier, I could have been a hero like dad was!" Anthony took a moment to simmer down before speaking again. "Dad would not be proud of me like this. If I had known earlier, I could have been somebody. I could have even gone with him!"

Darcy shook her head. "No, Anthony," she said.

"You're his son, and that's all that matters." Anthony sat back down. "There's something your father wanted you to have." She walked over to the closet where they stored grain. On the left wall of the closet there was a porous rock set deep into the stone. Darcy slid her hand into the wall and used the pores in the rock to pull it out. Instead of coming loose, when the rock was pulled mostly out of the wall, the entire side of the closet swung open. Anthony had never before seen a seam where the hidden door's edge met the closet wall, and he was even more surprised to see the secret room behind the door. It was like an old cellar, dank and dimly lit. "For years I've used this secret room to store our family's most treasured heirlooms and priceless antiques," Darcy said. Anthony looked at a cracked china plate on a shelf.

"If these are what we call priceless antiques, then it's no wonder that we're dirt poor," Anthony remarked.

"We may be poor financially, but we're rich in memories and heritage. Besides, there's more where that came from." She moved slowly to the back of the room. On that wall was something thing that looked better than gold to Anthony.

It was his father's old sword.

It was an expertly tempered length of silver steel that glinted in the light, with a hilt of actual gold welded onto the blade with extra care, and its pommel had a green emerald set into it.

"Your father told me to give it to you when you were near adulthood," his mother said. "He also wanted me to make sure you knew how to use it." For one of Anthony's birthdays his mom had found a book for beginner's level

swordsmanship. He had advanced to the intermediate level, but without a proper coach, he couldn't get much further. After Anthony slid it back into the decorated sheath, his mother brought out a wooden chest.

Inside the chest laid two items. One was what appeared to be a golden pocket watch, but on the side opposite the watch there was a compass. The second item, which was of much greater importance, was a rolled-up yellowed parchment. When Anthony unrolled the parchment, it was an elegantly detailed hand-drawn map of southeastern Interra, the insect-given name of the United States, from Anthony's colony all the way to the Great Hive.

"It will be much easier to find your way around with this map," Darcy said to Anthony as he continued packing food into his knapsack. When he was finished, Anthony engaged his mother in one last embrace.

"It's just so hard to lose you," his mother said.

"You're not losing me. I promise I'll be back," Anthony told her. With that he left, Artie following at his heels.

Darcy spoke sadly to herself, "That's what your father said."

Celia finished packing her supplies from her home. It was a lonely place—no pets and no relatives. As she often thought how lucky Anthony was, even if he couldn't see it. He lamented and grieved that he didn't have a father any longer, but at least he had a mother. Celia, however, had no one.

"Are we all ready?" Anthony asked Celia as they met at the main gate.

"As ready as we can be, I suppose," she replied. Gregorak came to bid them farewell.

"Travel safely, stay together, and with luck, I'll see you at the Hive," he said cheerily. As the two walked out of the gate, Anthony said to Celia, "I'm sorry to hear about your sculpture."

During the slavers' raid, her Agoz sculpture had been demolished when they had tried to cart it out of her art room.

"It's okay," she told him. If—I mean, *when*—we reach the Great Hive, I'll be able to rebuild it." And so Anthony and Celia, two aspiring adventurers, began their trek through uncharted territories.

Weaver's Trench

At the Vesthrax Hive, Queen Iriana stalked the many torture chambers of the prison block. Their desperate caterwauls were music to her ears. Of course, she liked to think of it as justice being served. Coincidentally, however, most of the prisoners either had simply crossed her, or were someone she held a grudge against.

Peering over the cathedral steeple, she caught a glimpse of the Great Hive. In comparison, her hive was severely dwarfed by the magnificent structure. She loathed the Hive for that reason (and for secret reasons she kept to herself). Blocking out the grim hymns echoing from inside the cathedral, Iriana began to assess her plan. Anyone else in Iriana's position (who shared Iriana's mindset) would probably try to destroy the Great Hive out of jealousy. However, despite how furiously she wished to do so, Iriana still wasn't nearly foolish enough to even consider such a feat. In fact, her true motive was not jealousy but vengeance.

It would be far wiser to bide her time, to wait for a diversion to create a path of opportunity to destroy her enemies. She had already taken care of all possible challengers: her pathetic mother, her sisters, and everyone else that might have squealed. (Half of them probably wouldn't have, but Iriana could be a very paranoid hornet.) In the midst of preparation for the Moon Festival, there would be a terrible accident. Once the Senate agreed with her plan, they would move in. You see, just before Queen Vespa's death, the Senate of the hive had begun to deteriorate, and with the confusion in the matter of selecting the new queen, much of the power was left with Iriana. Nobody would be stupid enough to disagree with her anyway.

At that point there would be two options: attack and enslave the occupants, or negotiate so that they would be lulled into a false sense of security, thus leaving them open for attack. If they decided to fight back, her army would have already taken over the surrounding towns and cities. Either way, she would win. Until then she would wait for when the opportunity arose. Creeping across the side of the groaning branch, Iriana returned to the hive.

Anthony and Celia had spent the last four hours trudging through the forest undergrowth with Artie scampering after them. "Anthony," Celia sighed, "how can we be sure this place even exists? The only—"

"Celia," he said irately, "I'm beginning to wonder if trav-

eling with you for a long-distance trek was worth missing the Moon Festival for." Celia shot back a sharp retort.

"*You're* the one who insisted on 'following your dreams' and taking us both on a journey through the wilderness without so much as a map!"

"I do *so* have a map!"

"Well, you sure can't read it!" Within a few more paces they reached a crossroad. In front of them was an old wooden sign with arrows. The arrow pointing to the left read, "Caris Creek, fifty yards." The other arrow, which pointed to the right, read, "Weavers' Trench, dead ahead."

"We should head for the river," Celia suggested. "Then we could collect more water and find fruits and berries."

"*I* think we should head for the trench," Anthony debated. "There's a clear path ahead, and we could find shelter for the night in the rotting tree stumps." The two ants glared at each other. As young insects, they had argued like this constantly back at their colony. Some things just never change.

They first tried the path to the creek, but the water was too treacherous. Anthony consulted his map, which showed a well-drawn-out footpath through the trench, although it was rugged terrain.

"It does seem that the trench would be our best option," Anthony told Celia smugly.

"Oh, all right," she capitulated. "But if we get caught by an orb weaver—"

"Relax," Anthony said calmly. "We just avoid the webs, and they don't bother us." Celia was referring to the golden silk orb weavers, particularly the species *Nephila clavipes*. They were notorious for preying on unwary travelers who

became ensnared in their webs and could become quite aggressive when disturbed, hence the ominous name, Weavers' Trench.

So Anthony and Celia continued right. As they ventured deeper into the trench, the brush began to thicken, and high above their heads, the trees seemed to bend inward. Soon less and less sunlight was visible through the dense underbrush, and the two were left traipsing cautiously through the dark, moist trench with nothing but the hand-drawn path on Anthony's map to guide them. In human proportions, the trench would be a fairly large ditch, with enough room for two compact cars to drive side by side. After another half hour of wandering along the path, Anthony and Celia had had enough. "We need to get a proper heading," Anthony said with exasperation. "We can't continue to wander aimlessly like this."

"How exactly do you propose we get a heading?" Celia asked skeptically. "I'm sure we wouldn't be able to see anything but brush for miles around."

"Well, I might as well try." Taking whimpering Artie in one arm, Anthony began using his other arms to climb up the trunk of the nearest tree.

"What do you see up there?" Celia called up as she made her way up the trunk.

"Come up here and see for yourself," Anthony called back down. One useful attribute of the ants is their skill and speed when it comes to climbing. In a few moments, Celia had scaled the trunk and joined Anthony on the topmost branch. As Celia had guessed, the trench ran on for almost a mile as it curved to the far right. But just

before the curve there were chains of towering magnificent buildings that shone in the sunlight like a diamond in the rough. "According to my map, that would be Regius City up ahead," Anthony told Celia, pointing at the map.

"It's pretty far from here," Celia pointed out. "How long do you think it would take us to get there?"

"Several days I'm sure, unless we're somehow able to find an alternative mode of transportation in this wilderness, like a grasshopper."

"And who's going to tame it?" asked Celia mockingly. "You? If it took you three months to teach Artie to roll over, how do you plan on controlling a wild grasshopper? And need I remind you that grasshoppers aren't the smartest creatures? They don't even speak basic insect!"

"Well, I guess not," Anthony admitted. "But we could buy one when we reach Regius City."

"In case you haven't noticed," Celia pointed out again, "we're a large species of ant. There wouldn't be enough room on its back for both of us to ride."

"Well then, we can buy two of them."

"Are you nuts? We could never afford that!"

"Must you contradict *everything* I say?" The duo argued back and forth on the branch, which unbeknownst to them, was rocking in the breeze. Artie nudged Anthony for attention but was ignored in the midst of the argument. Thunder rumbled, but the pair did not hear it. Gloomy gray clouds began rolling in, and finally there was a *plop* and yet another p*lop! Plop, plop, plop!* Anthony and Celia ceased their bickering for a moment and turned to see rain falling down in huge droplets. "We need to find shelter!" Celia shouted over the distant thunderclaps.

"Right, let's get out of here!" Anthony agreed. Anthony, Celia, and Artie made a beeline for the tree trunk. But as they began to climb down, a strong wind tore past their tree, throwing them off into the brush.

After Anthony recovered from the fall, he called out, "Celia, where are you?"

"I'm over here!" Anthony twisted his head to his right and found Celia sprawled out on the ground.

"Celia, where's Artie?" Anthony called to her worriedly.

"Up there," said Celia, jerking her head forward. Anthony looked up and saw Artie pacing under a dock leaf, trying to avoid the downpour.

"Don't worry, buddy. I'll help you in a minute," Anthony hollered up to Artie.

"Shh, don't talk so loud," Celia whispered nervously.

"How come?"

"Try to wiggle around," she told him simply. Anthony tried and finally noticed that their movement was being restricted. He also noticed that they weren't on the ground at all; in fact, they were still quite high up. And their movement was being restricted by an unpleasant silky filament that seemed quite unbreakable. It was a spider web.

"Well, we're in the web," Anthony noticed grimly. "So, where's the spider?"

"Trust me, you don't want to know."

Anthony heard it coming before he saw it. He heard its back brushing against the dangling leaves. He heard its hisses and clicks as it prepared to indulge in a hearty

snack. Then Anthony saw it. *That's one really big spider*, Anthony thought with dismay. *It must be a female.*

The ghastly beast slowly crept along the web, ready to inject her deadly venom into their intestines. The duo wiggled, lashed, bucked, and thrashed, Artie launched salvos of his sweet nectar secretion to divert the spider's attention from Celia and Anthony. She paid little attention. *This is the end,* Celia thought grimly. *We're both going to die trapped in a cocoon of cobwebs, dangling ten feet from the ground.* She thought of how horrified she was of heights. *Oh, the cruel irony!* On the dock leaf above them, Artie whimpered with concern for his best friend. The ever-nearing spider reared to strike. A jet of Artie's honeydew splashed upon Anthony and Celia's bodies, allowing Anthony to break free of the webbing. He sprang to the nearest twig, readied himself with a large pebble, and prepared to fight to the death. When Anthony had sprung away, the spider had overshot the lunge, sending her tumbling over the edge of the web.

No sign of the spider, Anthony thought to himself.

Celia screamed, "Anthony, look out!" Anthony saw the spider spiraling down upon him, suspended from a tree branch by a silk line. He hurled the pebble at the descending spider, striking it square in the forehead. She recoiled sharply before disconnecting the line, landing directly in front of Anthony with a *thump*. He drew his sword, holding it out in front of himself to prevent the spider from advancing. For the sake of steadiness, he straightened his many arm segments into two main parts, like a human

arm. She circled her prey slowly, Anthony following her every move. Then she attacked once again.

Anthony and the spider darted back and forth in a fierce competition to match the other's move. Anthony dodged nimbly away from her bites, lunges, and slashes; she recoiled from his thrusts while lashing out with her front pair of legs. Anthony tried to concentrate on sticking to the tree limbs, leaves, and twigs so as not to become stuck on the web. The pouring rain didn't seem to deter her advances, while Anthony stumbled and slipped, either due to the rain or his inexperience. The spider decided to retreat to a higher level, climbing up a web line. Anthony, Celia, and Artie watched the spider's movements carefully, waiting for her to climb back down. The pair watched her prepare to pounce.

The spider finally decided to come down upon Anthony's head. She launched herself at him from the perch, moving like a bolt of greased lightning. For Anthony, at that moment the whole world seemed to slow down. The spider sped slowly toward him, and like the beat of a hummingbird's wing, he swung twice, slicing her across the face before stabbing one of her eyes.

As the world sped up once again, the spider crashed through the web, landing with a splash in the mud below.

"Bravo, bravo! Most impressive," cheered a new voice from behind them. Anthony whipped around to face a large emperor dragonfly (*Anax imperator)* with eyes like blue-tinted saucers.

"How long have you been here?" Celia interrogated.

"Come on," the dragonfly urged, ignoring her question. "You look like you could use some rest."

A Brilliant Idea

Iriana paced restlessly in her quarters. She itched to begin her plot for conquest. It felt like ages since she had been deemed queen, and yet her ambition had increased tenfold. She had spent too much time clawing her way to the top to have to settle for a mere collection of unstable hives clustered within a rotting oak tree. Iriana wanted a grander territory to rule. *I'll have the empire that my sisters only dreamed of dominating*, she thought to herself. *Vespa was too afraid to do more than dream about it, but I have a plan.* Then she remembered the bees. Honeybees were easy prey for hornet-foraging parties near their nests. Where better to start her colonization?

"Squire," she called, "fetch the general. I've just had a brilliant idea." The timid page immediately scurried off to find him.

Several moments later the squire returned with the mighty general. "I've just returned with more food for the larvae," he announced. "What is your request, my liege?" General Razorwing was a large hornet who was the leader of the Vesthrax Armada and commander of the Lead Sting squad, a group of Iriana's elite forces. Being a male hornet, he was without a stinger, but he made up for it with single-minded determination and ferocity.

"General," Iriana briefed him, "I want you to gather a battalion of soldiers and raid the beehive on Zephyr's Knoll. Kill every bee, plunder every storeroom, and smite every pupa. For the glory of my coming empire, show no mercy."

Anthony, Celia, and Artie had taken refuge from the now rainy and windy weather in the dragonfly's humble cottage. It had been constructed from thistledown and bark, while the roofing consisted of palm fronds, and weeds and twigs served as building supports. "So, young ones," the elderly dragonfly asked, "what exactly is the nature of your journey?" Anthony and Celia then gave him a hurried explanation of how Anthony was convinced to travel to the Great Hive and be schooled in the ways of the Insect Champions. "I'm not surprised that Greg would suggest you going to the Great Hive. It's usually enigmatic youngsters like you that become great warriors in the future. And after seeing the way you handled your-

selves with that spider, you definitely seem like warrior material. By the way, my name's Omaha."

"I'm Anthony," Anthony said. "This is Celia, and that's Artie. Could you, by any chance, point us in the right direction? We're sort of lost."

"Hey," interrupted Celia, "what do you mean '*we*'?"

Anthony blushed embarrassedly.

"I'd be glad to help," Omaha said, trying to break the awkward silence. But what *would* they discover at their fabled destination? At the moment Anthony and Celia had a strong feeling that they weren't going to like it.

A Dark Secret

In a nearby beehive it was the busiest time of day. All around, workers were occupied with depositing nectar, tending to the queen's offspring, and sorting newborns into designated honeycomb slots. The entire complex was buzzing with activity. Suddenly, over the ramparts, the emergency alarm was sounded. Frantic swarms of terrified workers darted and scrambled for shelter. The unfortunate guards, however, did their best to bar the entryway to the incubation chamber, where a multitude of unprotected eggs laid. Yet above the screaming of the unsuspecting crowd, one voice cried a message of doom and destruction for the entire colony. "The hornets are approaching! The hornets are approaching!"

General Razorwing led his platoon into the beehive, each warrior toting the most deadly weapons he could muster. He himself was carrying his signature battle hammer, which could pierce the hide of an armored beetle. He scattered his warriors throughout the hive, hoping to cover as much ground as he could.

He earned his ominous nickname because of his renowned battle tactic, lining his wings with sharpened lead razors and then using them to rip through his opponents as he passed by. From his vantage point on a tree limb high above the hive, he shouted, "Hornets, move in! Capture the plaza! Take no prisoners!" General Razorwing then proceeded to bash the nearest honeybee with his hammer. His soldiers poured in upon the bees in endless waves, their war cries becoming thundering heralds of doom. Another squad of bees arrived and boxed General Razorwing in. He rounded on them suddenly, rushing his opponents. *Thwack*! General Razorwing cracked his target over the head and then dodged a dropkick from an advancing honeybee with a pirouette to the side. Before the next bee was able to respond, the general smote him with a mighty blow. He allowed his elite corps to dispatch the other warriors that were dogging him, that way he could engage in a crucial step in the raid.

Before him was a mammoth wooden gate guarding the hatching cells for the queen's eggs. He smote the petty militia barring his path with a series of tremendous swings and shoved the doors open. *Splotch*! General

Razorwing crushed a honeybee egg and tossed it aside. A countless amount of honeybees raced through the air to drive him out. He speared another egg, dodging a slash from a guard's sword. A particularly foolish guard flung himself onto the general's abdomen and was thrashed off by a fierce hammer strike. General Razorwing picked off a pair of approaching spear-bearing bees with a death spiral and then slammed another bee into the nearby wall.

But the general couldn't continue for much longer. There was much more of the enemy than he had surmised, and even more were pouring in every minute. "Coal bombs!" General Razorwing shouted to his elites before they soared away to a separate chamber. After several moments of no response from the elites, General Razorwing was becoming anxious.

"Fall back!" he roared to his soldiers. The wasps and hornets obeyed, drawing back toward the east side of the plaza. The front row of hornets lowered long pikes to keep the bees at bay. Above the bees, a row of tin war catapults rolled in, manned by heavily-padded hornets that had been waiting on the branches for the general's order. A crew of assisting hornets and wasps were busy packing coal into balls. Another team was igniting and then loading the hissing coals onto the catapults. "Fire one!" roared General Razorwing. The hive was bathed in an eerie scarlet light as crackling balls of coal rained down upon the line of bees. "Fire two!" he roared over the crashing. A second volley tore through the wooden gate and into the egg cells behind it. His troops rushed forward, cutting down the bees that hadn't been incinerated by the raining coal.

"Fan out!" General Razorwing shouted. A group of retreating bees was caught by a volley of spears. The conflagration had now spread in all directions through the higher levels of the hive, exterminating the remaining bees.

"Send some wasps to douse the flames," he told a lieutenant. "This hive is ours."

That evening, General Razorwing returned with his soldiers. "Status report," Queen Iriana prompted.

"We claimed victory swiftly and forcefully," General Razorwing replied, "with minimum casualties and minor difficulty."

"Excellent," she said. "But I'm not stopping with bees. You know where to go next," she said, tracing her finger across a map for emphasis. "Contact me for further instructions when the time is right." Before the general could ask when that was, she hovered away, deep into the fungus caverns. The fungus caverns were a nexus of damp twisting tunnels infested with odd-looking species of fungi. As Iriana ventured even deeper into the fungal labyrinth, she came to an abrupt halt at a sloping bed of moss, which ended at a small cave-like cell. Queen Iriana was the only one to have ever visited that cell, for it held a dark secret so horrible it could bring an end to her rule, or even worse, her *life*. Sliding away the ivy-laden gate that barred the opening, Iriana reached behind an angled spire on her crown and slipped out a small crystal vial that contained a revolting green liquid. Crouched on a crudely woven cot inside the cell was another hornet. Many scars lined her thorax

and abdomen, and she looked as if she hadn't bothered to wash herself for many days, perhaps a week. "Time for your medicine, *Ivy,*" Iriana crooned. The hornet on the cot focused her ocelli, the three small eyes embedded in her forehead, on Queen Iriana with burning animosity.

"Not this time, *Iri,*" she snapped in a slightly unsteady voice. Iriana was now panting with anger.

"*Never* call me that repulsive pet name again!" Iriana's sword was a blur of bronze as it swung over Ivy's head, missing by only a split second as Ivy twisted away. Ivy retaliated with a slash from a concealed bark shiv. Iriana knocked Ivy's blade away and bowled her over with a well-aimed kick. But she recovered quickly and leaped at Iriana, slashing at her face. Then Iriana managed to get hold of the hilt of Ivy's shiv and then twisted it from her grasp. Avoiding a jab from Ivy's sting, Iriana pinned her to the wall and shoved the vial to her mouth. Reluctantly accepting defeat, Ivy choked down the potion. Her legs buckled, and she collapsed with a shudder.

"Iriana," Ivy spoke in a quavering voice, "please end the madness. Don't do this to the kingdom. It's unjustified! You just can't do it!" Queen Iriana merely laughed.

"Not only *can* I do it, I already *am* doing it! And what you're doing is rotting away in a slimy dungeon." Ivy's sullen expression quickly transformed into a determined stare.

"I will escape this wretched pit, and you will be exposed for the treacherous monster you really are."

Stepping out of the cell, Iriana hissed, "You're joking, right? Look at what you've become. The kingdom's pride and joy? I don't think so." With another laugh, Iriana left.

That same afternoon, Anthony was preparing to spar with Omaha in the courtyard behind his house. "Are you sure about this?" Celia asked Anthony.

"Don't worry, I'll go easy on the old fellow," Anthony assured her. For an insect of his age, Omaha was quite spry. He could weave through the air, just out of Anthony's striking range, and then swoop down to catch Anthony off balance with a sequence of quick swipes. For safety, they used wooden twigs instead of actual blades.

"Stand your ground, Anthony! A warrior must be prepared to defend himself from any angle if needed." Omaha took to the skies, yet Anthony didn't spot him come down. Anthony paced the courtyard patiently. Then, from the fronds of a decaying palm, Omaha zipped through the air to strike Anthony. Anthony grabbed Omaha's right wing and steered him to the ground.

"Excellent, Anthony," he cried after they landed. "A fine method you've invented." Anthony walked off, satisfied. "But here's a tip for you." Anthony turned back in surprise. *Thwump*! He rolled over on his back, a sharp pain in his back. "Never leave a conscious foe with a weapon," Omaha finished. He took a silver shield from a weapon rack hidden behind an ivy trellis. Omaha grinned mischievously. "Now, let's have another go." Anthony hesitantly armed himself and began sparring.

Late that night, amidst the chorus of crickets, Anthony nursed his bruises in front of a crackling fire. Celia had hefted a bulky pan over the fire. The pan had been filled with three fresh kernels of corn.

"So, how did 'going easy on the old fellow' work out?" Celia questioned him, stifling a laugh.

"Shut up," Anthony groaned. He peeked inside the rapidly heating pan. "Why are you wasting perfectly good corn, anyway?"

"Omaha taught me this. He said that when the kernels are hot enough, they're supposed to—" *Pop*! *Pop-pop*! *Pop*! The steaming kernels exploded, leaving three warm white puffs in the pan.

"It's beautiful," Anthony sighed. He skewered the lightweight puff on a stick and began munching with relish.

"Itff deliciouff," Celia declared with a full mouth.

"And it's called *popcorn*," Omaha chimed in, lifting the third kernel out of the pan with his own stick. "It's a trick I learned from the humans. Some of them have camped out here before." He took another bite. "I've done some thinking about where you two said you were going, and it would take awfully long to get there on foot." Anthony and Celia moaned in unison. "Therefore, I have taken the liberty of arranging an alternate method of travel for the two of you." The pair perked up at this.

"How will we be traveling?" Anthony queried.

"That isn't important right now," Omaha replied casually. "Anyway, I've gotten you both something for your quest." He laid out two objects in front of the fire: a length

of silvery rope of some sort and a glass jar filled with a thick, reeking, brown slime.

"Yuck, what is that nasty stench?" Celia asked in disgust, her antennae twisting with displeasure.

"That disgusting odor is the smell of spider oil." Omaha chuckled. "It is the natural material on any spider's body that keeps it from becoming stuck on its own web. The silvery threadlike material is a rope woven from a spider's webbing. I had it custom-made by the spider itself after I found her lost egg sack in a rainstorm. This webbing is six times stronger than steel of the same density, allowing it to hold fast to anything it's tied around." Anthony and Celia ran the rope through their hands in awe. Six times stronger than *steel*! Imagine the possibilities.

"Now, perhaps we should return to the subject of travel," suggested Omaha. "When you exit the trench from right *here*," he said, pointing to the northeast part of the trench on Anthony's map, "and enter Regius City at the main gate, there should be a tunnel to Zephyr's Knoll from the city hall courtyard. Follow the creek north, and it should lead you to Bullfrog Bayou. Head northwest from the bayou on the trail that will take you through Rindou Forest, and you should reach the Great Hive, safe and sound." Omaha, Anthony, and Celia took a few minutes to finish their popcorn before speaking. "Say," Omaha said, "how about you two camp out here, under the stars."

"That sounds like a pleasant idea." Celia yawned. Anthony and Omaha removed the pan and doused the fire.

"Well, g'night you two," Omaha said sleepily. "I'll see you in the morning, with your flight vehicles all ready."

FluffFlight Commercial Airlines

The next morning, in the echoing comb corridors of the Hive of Vesthrax, Queen Iriana was performing one of a hornet queen's most intense, painful responsibilities: performing consecutive periods of near-constant labor. She would scale the porous comb walls, depositing the eggs one by one into each empty cell, producing new (mostly female) children for the hive. *How on earth did Mother put up with this?* Iriana thought to herself, sweat pouring from her forehead as she deposited yet another egg. "At least it'll hurt less by tomorrow," she assured herself. After releasing another egg, the perpetual flow seemed to halt. Iriana breathed a sigh of relief, and she hovered back to

her throne at the end of the cell hall. She breathed heavily, waiting for the aching in her abdomen to cease.

"Excuse me, Your Highness?"

"What is it?" Iriana snapped back. The guard drew back, surprised by the queen's hostility.

"Your Highness, the central main branch is on fire."

Iriana launched herself from the nearest window and flew to the right main branch, where she could see the fire raging up the dry bark. Wasps and hornets with pails of water rushed over to quench the inferno. The sun was bright that day, and the ancient oak tree's dry, waxy leaves had ignited in the intense heat. The fire was soon extinguished, leaving the central main branch's bark steaming and charred. After watching the fire, Iriana had formulated an ingenious plan. In her perspective, the disaster had come at a very "convenient" time.

After the fire, the Hive Senate had held council to discuss the nature of the tree's health. Two members from each of the tree's eight hives (all forming the united Vesthrax Hive) were present at the meeting. The current topic of discussion was measures that could be taken to prevent further similar incidents. A wasp from Hive One began. "Our ancient home, beloved as it may be, has become quite vulnerable to natural hazards and other agents of destruction. We were fortunate not to sustain any casualties during the recent fire on the central main branch, but I believe the Senate must work on a practical solution for the benefit of the hive's well-being." The Senate applauded this statement. Queen Iriana was the next to speak.

"I am glad to inform the Senate that I have devised a solution for protecting the hive population. I find that the best way to keep current and future generations of our wasps and hornets is to spread it out." There were murmurs of interest among the senators. "This, of course," she continued, "would require more territory." Iriana produced a long scroll from the pocket of her flowing silk robe. "This is my proposition. Read it well, and if you wish to support it, I'll just require your signatures on the dotted line."

Iriana's proposition, which was accepted with a unanimous decision by the Senate, was read by criers across the hive as follows:

> **Colonization Act Twelve**
> By decree of Her Highness, Queen Iriana of the noble Hive of Vesthrax, and by unanimous agreement of the Hive Senate, Colonization Act Twelve shall hence be enacted. Her Highness has issued a call for military cooperation from the Vesthrax Grand Army to make negotiations with surrounding territories that are to be colonized. All negotiations are to remain entirely peaceful until faced with violent opposition from the province to be colonized, in which case military retaliation will be executed. A military campaign may be initiated in case of severe rebellion. The colonization will go into effect throughout much of southeastern Interra and will progress at the Queen's discretion.

"This hive, our holy land, is a flower that has yet to blossom," Iriana had told the Senate, her silver tongue licking away their doubt. "It is a bud containing the elixir of life. That bud is like a fresh pinecone. All it requires is a little fire to singe away its sap coating.

"If we expand, as a pinecone's seeds are released by fire, we can harness our elixir of life and share it with those around us. By sowing the seeds of opportunity, we shall reap its fruits."

Iriana was highly satisfied at her accomplishment. After the act was signed, the general was informed. "Where shall we begin?" General Razorwing asked her.

"Regius City is the closest nearby. We shall begin there. I will leave for the city early tomorrow morning. If all goes well, there shall be no need for bloodshed. If not," she grinned at the general, "then don't hesitate to react."

On the same morning as the fire, Anthony and Celia had risen from their semi-sleep with an uneasy sensation in the pits of their stomachs. This stemmed from Omaha's comment that they would be using flight vehicles to reach Regius City. What sort of flight vehicles? Neither of the two had ever experienced flight, and they weren't sure of exactly how much they would enjoy it.

Anthony and Celia marched up to Omaha's house and found that he was waiting for them. "It's about time you two got here," he told them. "Follow me." Anthony and Celia grabbed their supplies and left the house again.

Omaha brought them to a hill behind his house, which seemed entirely ordinary, except for one thing.

"Look at the size of those dandelions!" Anthony shouted over the wind swishing through the grass. On the hill was a grove of massive dandelions, each roughly six inches high.

"This is how I make a living!" Omaha proclaimed. "I call it FluffFlight Commercial Airlines. The seeds on this one"—he prodded a dandelion in the center—"are barely two inches long, just enough to support your weight. The wind today is perfect for a one-way trip to Regius City!" Anthony and Celia unpacked without a moment to lose. They unloaded their belongings into separate sacks, which were tied onto a caravan of seeds that Anthony would pull along with a rope. Omaha then tied Anthony and Celia onto seeds of their own, and they were ready for takeoff. Before they took flight, Omaha handed Anthony a sling bag heavy with money.

"Thank you," said Anthony, "for everything. Even the beating."

"You both need this money more than I do. Are you ready for takeoff?" Anthony and Celia nodded. "The winds will take you directly to Regius City. Farewell, and have a safe journey!" Omaha threw his weight against the dandelion, and the seeds were released. Anthony and Celia were carried high, high up into the air, Weavers' Trench disappearing quickly beneath them.

"This is amazing!" Celia cried to Anthony.

"I'm flying!" Anthony whooped. It was such an exhilarating feeling—a feeling of freedom, being one with the air,

and soaring wherever the wind blew them. They were gliding through damp clouds, feeling the wind whip through their antennae. "Wait a minute... where's Artie?"

"Relax, he's in your backpack," Celia assured him. Artie was enjoying the flight from the safety of his master's backpack, sticking his head out of the zipper to feel the wind. A gaggle of geese flew so close that Anthony and Celia were tickled by their soft feathers. They whirled over trees, over the ominous sprawl of Weavers' Trench, unaware in their ecstasy that their fantastical journey was coming to an end.

"I think we're losing altitude!" Celia shouted to Anthony.

"I think you're right!" Anthony shouted back, struggling to keep control of their airborne caravan of luggage. "We must be getting nearer to the city!" All at once, the air seemed to slip out from under them. Anthony and Celia found themselves diving like falcons while their seeds continued to spin like dervishes of down feathers. Soon the two were back on solid ground, the trees towering above them once more.

Celia noticed that the ground they were standing upon was a neat cobblestone path. Just a few feet before them stood an ornate wrought-iron gate. Anthony and Celia untied themselves and their luggage and let the seeds float away. They started forward, knowing full well what awaited them beyond the gate. They had reached Regius City.

Learning How to Ride

It was dark, dank, and chilly where Ivy was. It always had been. Ivy struggled just to move herself. She strenuously hauled herself onto her back. It was her sister's fault, of course. *She can take away my throne, my name, and even my dignity, but she* cannot *take away my spirit*, Ivy thought to herself. *Ivy is not my name. I am Princess Vespa the Second, and that title is something that my sister can never take away!*

Regius City was a marvelous sight to behold for Anthony and Celia. Romanesque buildings lined the busy streets—restaurants and shops of all kind as far as the eye could see.

Anthony and Celia wandered down the streets, their eyes filled with awe. Artie scampered excitedly around them, exchanging greetings with other nearby pets. There was only one problem: what were they going to do next? They looked inside the sling bag to investigate what Omaha had left them.

In the bag were three trins, four fordes, five bicartas, twenty cartas, and forty crests, which would have been comparable to one thousand human dollars. Anthony and Celia weren't sure what to do with their enormous amount of spending money.

"Where could we start?" Anthony asked eagerly.

"Maybe we should ask for directions first," Celia suggested. They stopped in front of a country villa estate, where a stately flower mantis passed by. Before Celia could stop him from doing so, Anthony approached the mantis.

"Excuse me, ma'am," Anthony began in his most polite tone of voice, "but we are travelers on a long journey. Are there any places in the area that could suit our needs?" The mantis was obviously of high class, so Celia was surprised when she pointed out to Anthony the barn behind them.

"Oh no," Celia said firmly. "Uh-uh, definitely not, absolutely *no way*!"

The sign above the barn read, "Nobility Stables: Fine breeders of Orthoptera for forty-five years."

Anthony and Celia entered the barn, Anthony's eyes wide with awe at the many species of grasshoppers, crickets, and locusts. Celia's antennae wrinkled with disgust at the stenches flowing from each stall. Artie squeezed under the gate of one stall and scampered back out hurriedly as a locust snapped at him. A short, stocky British pill bug rolled over to them from another line of stalls.

"My name is Pao," he introduced himself. "Welcome to Nobility Stables. How can I help you?"

"Hello, my name is Anthony, my friend next to me is Celia, and my friend whom your locust almost ate is called Artie. We are traveling a great distance and need two of your fastest breed to get us there."

"My creatures do not come cheap, you know."

"Any price we're willing to pay," said Celia.

"Very well then. Follow me." The pill bug led them past the locust stalls and brought them to the back of the barn. Pao measured Anthony's height (roughly half an inch) and weight and then Celia's. He thought for a moment before leading the two outside. Pao first returned with a chestnut-brown house cricket for Celia. "*Acheta domesticus*," he told her. "Her name is Alba." Pao tied Alba to a pole beside the barn doors and returned inside.

He exited this time with a bright green migratory grasshopper just longer than Celia's cricket, with speckles of blue on its wings. "*Melanoplus sanguinipines*," Pao told Anthony. "His name is Tramonto."

Pao saddled and bridled Tramonto and Alba, then taught Anthony and Celia how to mount them by grabbing the bridles and swinging themselves onto the saddles. "Do you know how to ride?" Pao asked them.

"No, but we were hoping you could teach us," said Anthony.

"Of course!" Pao answered cheerily. "And for you two, there'll be no extra charge."

Pao led them to a pasture a yard away from his barn, where he trained the nymphs of grasshoppers, crickets, and locusts. Anthony and Celia sat on their steeds as Pao led them so they would become used to their position on the saddles. Tramonto was mild mannered and gave Anthony little trouble, while Alba, being younger and more energetic, required a more firm hand from Celia. Once in the pasture, Pao began instructing them.

"A rider must make use of his or her natural aids—hands, legs, the seat, and most importantly, voice. These two fine steeds have been trained to hop when given the verbal signal 'luppolo.' You may use gentle taps with your feet to get them to speed up. In order to slow them down, say 'ridurre,' and stop them completely by tugging on the bridle. Now, let's begin riding, shall we?"

Anthony and Celia began with fence jumping. They encouraged Tramonto and Alba to gain speed and slapped them on their sides when they neared the fence. Anthony soared gracefully over, although he fell off when Tramonto landed. Celia also managed to clear the fence but was thrown off of the saddle on the landing.

Hopper-back, cricket-back, and locust-back riding are harder to master than horseback riding because their gallops are entirely different. With each gallop, they take a medium-length hop, making for a constantly jostling ride, unless the steed is capable of flight, which is the case of locusts during swarm season. But after a few more runs, Anthony and Celia could glide effortlessly on their steeds'

backs. “Well done!” Pao congratulated them. “You’re riding is superb. But there is still the matter of payment. They both cost three fordes each. ”

“No problem,” Anthony said, handing him the gold coins.

“Enjoy your stay in Regius City!” Pao called to them as they rode off.

They rode back into Regius City, Tramonto and Alba trotting down the streets, with Artie clinging to Tramonto’s saddle. They halted Tramonto and Alba in Fountain Square, which was surrounded by shops, restaurants, and inns. “It’s getting late,” Celia noticed. “We need to find a place where we can spend the night.”

“Like where?” Anthony asked her.

“How about there?” Celia pointed to a building right across from the square. Its sign read, “The Fountain Side Suites: Vacant suites for only one trin per night.”

“That looks like a nice place to stay,” Anthony said. A firefly valet at the entrance took Tramonto and Alba to the stables behind the hotel. Before retiring to their suite, Anthony and Celia enjoyed the greatest dining experience Regius City had to offer, at La Restaurant Raffine. Celia relished the decadent mussel strips with clam sauce, while Anthony indulged himself with fried shrimp puffs. Seafood was one of the most expensive of insect delicacies, and never before had Anthony or Celia been able to gorge freely on it.

“Oh, sweet shrimp,” Anthony whispered to his meal. “Where have you been all my life?”

After the shrimp, however, Anthony did not share in Celia’s second course of buttered escargot. In fact, he had become strangely silent.

Celia stopped slurping up her second course long enough to ask, "What's wrong, Anthony? You haven't touched your snail." Anthony seemed to snap out of his trance.

"What? Oh, sorry, I was j-just thinking of my mom. I wonder how she's doing. I hope the colony's recovered from the slavemaker ants' attack. I wonder what she'd think of me now. Eating seafood in a fancy restaurant? Ha!" Celia and Anthony laughed together. When they were finished, Celia discussed the next day with him.

"Where do we plan on going first tomorrow?" she asked Anthony.

"Probably city hall, I guess. We could stop at a few detours along the way if anything interests us." When their glowworm waitress returned, they paid her for the dinner and climbed the staircase to their suite.

The suite itself was marvelous. The room sported luxurious furniture and two queen-sized beds and a balcony that looked over Fountain Square. "Well, it's been a long day." Anthony yawned. "I think we'd better call it a night."

"I agree," Celia said, flopping onto her bed.

"Man, these mattresses are like clouds," Anthony said as he pulled the bedcovers over himself. Celia followed suit, Artie lay on the edge of Anthony's bed, and they soon were drifting off to La-la Land. While Celia and Artie enjoyed a restful night, Anthony, on the other hand, spent most of his time pacing back and forth on silent feet, trying to piece together the easiest possible route from the city. After grumbling angrily in frustration for his own uncertainty, he collapsed back on his bed, still restless.

Iriana, meanwhile, had taken a late-night flight to our heroes' same location. Flying in the cool night air refreshed Iriana and helped her organize her thoughts. The folds of her purple silk cloak flapped wildly behind her like a pair of bat wings. When she reached the city, Iriana circled it twice to make sure no one was awake, for fear that someone might spot her. By the time she landed, her wings felt like lead. *I need to rest somewhere*, she thought to herself.

She staggered to the door of the nearest inn in sight. Iriana opened the door and stumbled inside and ... *Wait*, she realized. *The door was unlocked.* On the door were slashes forming the later *R. Razorwing*, she thought with a grin. *If he can break into a high-security hotel this easily, it's a wonder we haven't already taken the city.* She stalked up the staircase with expert stealth, avoiding loose floorboards that would surely creak.

When Iriana located yet another door marked with the letter R, she threw herself onto the king-size straw bed inside. "I have a glorious day tomorrow," she told herself. "Great things will happen, and I will reap the benefits."

Dangerous Knowledge

"Hurry up, will ya?" Celia called to Anthony. It was a bright sunny morning in Regius City, and Anthony had stopped at two detours so far on their way to city hall.

Celia tapped her feet impatiently outside of the armory while Artie marked his territory, next to Alba's foot. Alba kicked out, bowling the aphid over. "Knock it off, you two," she scolded them. She called to Anthony again, "Are you *almost* done?"

"All right, all right, sheesh." Anthony stepped out of the armory, brandishing his new shield. It was a plain, semi-triangular piece of steel without any sort of crest or symbol. "So," Anthony inquired, twirling it, "how does it look?"

"It's all right, if you like that sort of thing. Now, could we move along?" They set off again toward city hall, and yet again, Anthony needed to stop.

"*Another* bathroom break?" Celia moaned.

"Of course not," Anthony answered. He rushed to a vendor and returned with a jelly-filled doughnut. He tossed a bit to Artie, who devoured it happily. "Now I'm all set," Anthony said with a full mouth. Within fifteen minutes they had navigated through the upper city and found city hall.

City hall was the most magnificent, elaborate building Anthony and Celia had ever seen. It was a sprawling Parthenon-inspired complex, built by a workforce of Greek ants centuries before. It was constructed almost entirely of peach-red alabaster, the color of dawn. The columns on all four sides of the enormous structure were intricately ornamented with painstakingly detailed designs, and the roofs were sloped and irregular like anthills. Anthony and Celia entered the lobby, feeling dwarfed by the massive building. They were equally intimidated inside.

The lobby was bustling with activity, not dissimilar from the city streets. Dignitaries, nobility, and all classes of important insects strutted throughout the halls. Celia asked a tsetse fly secretary about directions to the city hall courtyard. Anthony stood in the center of the spherical lobby, watching the comings and goings of other insects. All of them, however, lived in the city and had no idea how to leave the city other than through the main gate. Hopefully someone else there did.

Out of nowhere a tall figure, roughly twice Anthony's height and dressed in a flowing purple silk cloak shoved past him. Under the hood, all that could be seen were

two antennae, and under the cloak was a bulge where the abdomen was. *The nerve*, Anthony thought huffily. He stuffed the half-eaten remains of his jelly doughnut into a pocket on his belt. Anthony was surprised to see the crowd of important-looking insects part as the hooded figure passed through. Celia rushed over to Anthony.

"I saw what happened back there. Some of those upper-class insects have some nerve, don't they. Anthony?" Anthony snapped out of his daze.

"Huh? Oh, yeah. You know, I can't shake the feeling that something bad is going on. In fact, I think I'll go check things out." Celia pulled him back as he began following the strange figure.

"Anthony, listen to me. Don't get dragged into something you don't understand. You have no idea what sort of trouble you might get yourself into."

"Well, I guess I won't know until I get into trouble, will I?" Anthony replied wryly. Making sure that no one else was looking, he pulled a grate loose from a stone heating duct connected to the boiler room. Before Celia could stop him, he crawled in, heading in the direction the hooded figure had gone. Artie peered in after his swiftly escaping master. He cocked his head inquisitively at Celia.

"Oh, it's really nothing, Artie. Anthony's just going to get us killed…or worse." She sighed. "Why did I ever leave the colony?"

Meanwhile, in the stone duct Anthony crawled on all six legs, as he would have when mining a narrow niche back at his colony. He peered through the occasional grate, catching glimpses of the stranger he was trailing. The stranger reached a door with a sign that read, "Mayor Ferdinand's Office."

The two guards at the door stepped aside for the stranger to pass through. Anthony climbed an upward duct and was soon in the mayor's ceiling.

The stranger approached the mayor's desk with a purposeful stride. "I'm very busy today," the plump tick said without looking up from his work. "Please schedule an appointment before coming to my office."

"I don't *need* an appointment, Ferdinand," the stranger hissed in a voice that reminded Anthony of winter frost. As the mayor looked up, the stranger removed the hood; it was a female hornet with a mother-of-pearl tiara on her head.

"Why, Your Majesty, I d-didn't know that... I mean, I didn't expect that you—"

"Save your apologies, Ferdinand. I didn't come for small talk." *A queen!* Anthony thought in surprise. *What could* she *have come here for?* Below him, the hornet kept talking. "Listen up, and listen closely, because I'm going to make you an offer you can't refuse.

"Up until now your city has been independent from other kingdoms or alliances. I've come here intent on changing that."

"Why is my city of interest to you?" Mayor Ferdinand asked, somewhat anxiously.

"I felt I could confide my greater ideals to you. Your city is closest to my hive, so cooperation would be easier. Now, my plans are as follows..."

Iriana poured out the most convoluted details of her plan. She figured she could trust Ferdinand, not really because she thought he could keep a secret well, but more because he would be too afraid to tell anyone. "And so you see," Iriana said when she was finished, "all that is required of you is to *sign this paper*." She unraveled a scroll from her cloak, which the mayor read with growing distaste.

"I don't understand," Mayor Ferdinand said, shaken. "How could you even consider hostilities against such a benevolent power as the Great Hive?"

"For my own reasons," Iriana snapped back at him, "which you have no business sticking your nose into. So are you going to cooperate *or not*?" The mayor leaned in closer.

"Iriana, your plans are despicable. Ideas like these are dangerous, and with them you threaten the tranquility of a peaceful land. I shall have no part in this blasphemous scheme!" Iriana shook with rage. "You will rue the day you scorned me, Ferdinand! I will see to it that your entire city shall pay for your folly!" As she began to storm out of the room, she stopped. Her antennae twitched, catching a sweet scent. *Jelly doughnut?* She traced the scent to a stone heating duct in the ceiling. She looked through the grate to find the source... and met Anthony's gaze.

Anthony pulled away from Iriana's glare and at once crawled back through the ducts, unaware that Iriana was tracking him on all six legs. Anthony had heard terrible things back in the ceiling of the mayor's office, things that made him cringe just thinking of them, things that he hadn't wanted to hear. Unfortunately for Anthony, Iriana hadn't wanted anyone else to hear it either.

When he crawled out of the loose grate back in the lobby, neither Celia nor Artie was waiting for him, but Iriana was. As Anthony was peeking out of the duct, Iriana grabbed him by the throat and began throttling him. Iriana held Anthony by his neck and abdomen, cutting off air flow to the spiracles he used to breathe. He gasped for breath as she twisted him as one might twist a wet cloth. "What did you hear?" Iriana interrogated Anthony.

"Nothing, I-I mean I didn't know, Your Majesty; it was a—"

"Don't patronize me, worm! What gave you the gall to intrude upon my private conversation, you sniveling maggot? I'll ask you but one more time. *What did you hear*?" Celia ran back into the lobby just to see Iriana tormenting poor Anthony.

"Hey, get your hands off of him!" she shouted at Iriana. Artie followed her, snarling angrily at Iriana as she strangled Anthony. Iriana, not amused by their attempt to rescue Anthony, drew her sword. She pointed it at Celia's face as she rushed forward and kicked Artie away as he prepared to latch onto her heel. Celia stood stock still, her gaze riveted on the menacing sword tip wavering just above her eyes.

"Learn your place, wench, or you shall share your friend's punishment." She turned to Anthony, who was in a critical condition. "This is the price you pay for interfering with events beyond your control."

"But I wasn't interfering!" gasped Anthony feebly. He didn't dare to try to escape to reach his sword, for both Iriana's size and strength were far greater than his own. Indeed, Iriana was a whopping *two inches* in length, a startling size, even for a queen. "It was just … um … curiosity," he choked desperately.

"Curiosity killed the caterpillar," scolded Iriana, "and it's about to kill you!" She wrenched Anthony cruelly to the point where he feared that he might be torn in half.

Celia could stand no more of it. To the astonishment of the spectators who had surreptitiously gathered about the three of them, she threw herself onto the distracted Iriana and stung her.

At that point everything became a blur of activity and sound for Anthony. Iriana howling with pain, Celia pulling him through the crowd, insects scattering with confusion, Artie licking his face—everything swirled about him in a vortex of mayhem.

And then it all went black.

Iriana swore with agony amid the confusion. She rubbed the sore spot on her abdomen where the ant girl had stung her. *Insolent wretch*, she thought bitterly. *I shall make her* and *the eavesdropping interloper pay*. Iriana produced a whistle from her cloak and blew into it until her face turned blue. A return call from a bugle sounded from outside after several moments. General Razorwing crashed through a dusty window that cast dull shafts of light into the lobby. He approached Iriana amid the shattered glass and cowering insects.

"I assume that not everything went well, my queen," he addressed her upon entering. Iriana's answer to his question was clear enough.

"Raze the city to the ground!" she roared with fury. *And the two meddling ants shall burn with it*, she thought with satisfaction.

When Anthony awoke, Celia was dragging him swiftly down the alabaster corridors of city hall. "What happened?" he moaned wearily. His whole body felt sore and cramped, especially around his midsection.

"No time to explain," Celia panted. We need to get out of here as fast as possible, or else—"

Celia was interrupted by a deafening crash from the roof. Rubble rained down upon them, and crowds of screaming, panicking insects scrambled past them. "Too late," Celia sighed.

"What about Tramonto and Alba?" Anthony eked out.

"They're right behind us." The grasshopper and the cricket came hopping in, frightened by the loud explosions outside. Several more booms rocked city hall.

"What've I done?" Anthony groaned. His head lolled back.

"Anthony? Stay with me now, c'mon." They stopped at an intersection of three hallways. Celia was utterly stumped. "Which way do we go?"

"I think we should go in the opposite direction of the loud booms," Anthony said.

"Good idea. I'm not sure what exactly is making all of the commotion, and I certainly don't want to find out, especially if that awful hornet has summoned reinforcements, which she probably has. Pray tell me, what exactly was she so riled about?" *Boom*, *Boom*!

"There's no time to talk; just put me on Tramonto and don't stop running." Celia tossed Anthony onto Tramonto's saddle, and he weakly gripped the bridle. *Boom*, *Boom*, *Boom*!

They made off at a dash, not daring to look behind them as the booming grew louder and rubble continued to collapse from the ceiling. After climbing a short staircase, Celia leaped to the nearest window to investigate the explosions. The room was flooded with dancing, flickering orange lights when she pulled back the drapes.

"Uh-oh."

With ecstasy, Iriana watched Regius City burn. *That ought to teach those insufferable imbeciles to defy my brilliance.* She perched atop the fountain of Fountain Square, watching her grenadiers bombard city hall.

Indeed, her MR&D (Military Research and Development) department had concocted an ingenious warfare device. They called it the "quartz cluster." It was a unique variant of hand grenade with a deadly mechanism. When a grenadier squeezed the curved grip (instead of pulling out a ring), the friction caused by the resulting turning of gears would ignite the sack of gunpowder nestled inside. The explosion would release the quartz packed around the sack, sending flaming shards of quartz flying in all directions. The assault on Regius City was proving to be a most effective testing stage for the weapons. Just then General Razorwing arrived, pulling Iriana out of her diabolical reveries.

"Few of the city's inhabitants continue to resist us, my queen," he reported. "But those who do are not showing any signs of capitulation. What shall you have us do?"

"Their resistance shall be short lived," Iriana predicted with confidence. "Make an example out of them, one that none shall ever forget. Teach them to fear the insurmountable will of my new empire." The general began to hover away. "And by the way," she added, "in the future, negotiations may be of no use to us. In case other provinces and kingdoms react like Regius City, force should be used firsthand." General Razorwing grinned broadly in anticipation of a new campaign. Iriana flew over to city hall, which was swiftly becoming engulfed in flames.

"You are going inside, my liege?" General Razorwing asked nervously.

"Indeed,"—Iriana unsheathed her sword and stroked it menacingly—"for I have a quarry that I do not intend on letting escape my sting."

Anthony and Celia were finding it increasingly difficult to navigate the quickly burning city hall. At one point in their

befuddled trek, an entire section of the roof collapsed in on them, leaving a gap where sunlight shined through.

"Look out!" Anthony hollered as Celia walked under the gap. She jumped away just in time, as a rotund wooden barrel dropped in, drenching the entire hallway—and them—in a foul-smelling liquid.

"It's gasoline!" Celia cried. "That's what is spreading the flames so quickly!"

Sure enough, a quartz cluster followed the barrel. Upon landing, it exploded, sending flaming shards of quartz blasting in all directions. Anthony and Celia ducked to avoid the shrapnel, Anthony throwing his arms over Artie to protect him. Unfortunately, when they set off again, Tramonto was limping, a chunk of quartz embedded in his right hind leg.

"It'll be okay, boy," Anthony assured Tramonto. Things, however, really weren't okay for them. And they were about to get a whole lot worse, as a cold, mocking voice drilled into their skulls

"I hope you're not leaving the party already." Iriana laughed from behind a curtain of flame. "You're both just in time for the main event!" Iriana pounced from the flames with a spine-chilling cackle. Anthony hopped away on Tramonto just in time to escape her stinger. Celia followed suit on Alba, and they both galloped away. "You can run, but you can't hide!" Iriana cried after them.

It was true; there was nowhere for Anthony or Celia to hide from the murderous hornet queen. Despite the billowing clouds of noxious smoke, nothing could shake Iriana from her prey. But finally there emerged from the conflagration a ray of hope: the exit to the city hall courtyard.

The courtyard was a circular outdoor enclosure surrounded by stone, forming a cylindrical pit. Covering that expanse of stone opposite from city hall was a sprawling bougainvillea with thick, thorny vines decorated with magenta flowers. Cradled within the massive plant was the cave-like entrance to the tunnel that would lead them to Zephyr's Knoll.

Anthony and Celia dismounted Tramonto and Alba, who bounded up the vines to the narrow tunnel entrance. Anthony scooped up Artie in his arms and used his two pairs of legs to do all the climbing for him. It was a strenuous business for Anthony and Celia to haul themselves up the thorny bougainvillea vines, but they were more concerned at the moment with escaping Iriana.

"We're almost halfway to the top, Anthony!" Celia hollered up to Anthony after roughly twenty-five minutes of climbing. Strangely, their pursuer was nowhere to be seen. But then Iriana hurtled out of nowhere, zooming toward Anthony at a breakneck speed. Anthony took a leap of faith and landed on a thorny ledge just higher from where he stood earlier. Letting Artie scale the rest of the wall himself, Anthony stood up and drew his sword.

Iriana only laughed. "Going to fight me, are you? Very well, then." Iriana became a whirlwind of twirling purple cloak and slashing bronze sword. Anthony saw that he could not match her superior combat skills, and he was unable to deflect each of her blows.

"Not so confident now, are you, *Anthony*?" Iriana hissed.

"Going to run while you still can?" Anthony had no choice. But when he looked down the vines, he did not see Celia.

"Anthony, catch!" Celia's voice rang out. Anthony reached upward and caught one end of the length of spider web rope that Omaha had given to them. And without thinking, Anthony jumped. Knowing that Celia had a firm grip on the opposite end of the rope, he swung onto a small rock ledge before he began climbing. When Iriana flew over to intercept him, Anthony swung away once again and resumed climbing.

This process continued until Anthony was safely to the tunnel entrance, one step ahead of Iriana. But she would not be denied her vengeance. Iriana darted forward in a maddened frenzy, her sword aimed at Anthony. However, Celia would not see him slain by this ruthless hornet. She lassoed an overhanging vine with the spider web rope and yanked down with all of her might. It collapsed upon Iriana just as she had perched in front of them, and they ran off laughing with Tramonto, Alba, and Artie as she struggled to free herself.

"You may have escaped this time, but you haven't seen the last of me … and you can *count on that*!"

Back at what used to be Regius City, Iriana returned to her soldiers chagrined and spiteful. After she recounted her defeat to General Razorwing, she demanded that he bring forth a cunning, dependable officer to her.

He returned with Lieutenant Harquebus.

Harquebus was, as a yellowjacket, not physically

imposing. But he made up for his slim, wiry features with a cunning that Iriana had seen only in herself. She briefed him on his mission. "Lieutenant Harquebus, take your platoon of twenty or so soldiers and track down two ants. They are public enemies of the glorious Hive of Vesthrax and must be stopped at all costs before they can reach the Great Hive. They have taken the courtyard tunnel to Zephyr's Knoll, the site of the general's earlier conquest over the recalcitrant bees. Find them and slaughter them in any manner you can think of. This is your mission, Harquebus. I expect you to fulfill it."

"I assure you, Your Majesty," Harquebus answered, "that they shall not live to see the Hive."

Part Two: The Chase

The Secrets of the Knoll

Anthony, Celia, Tramonto, Alba, and Artie celebrated their victory over Iriana joyously as they navigated the tunnel to Zephyr's Knoll.

"But it was *your* quick thinking that saved the day," Anthony insisted to Celia. "I wouldn't have made it here without you.

"Oh, you're too much," Celia thanked him, blushing. "But I have to ask, what *did* you hear in that duct?" The jubilant mood quickly melted away.

"I heard terrible things," Anthony muttered. "I heard things about death, conquest, war, and some things that may already have happened. I know that now there can't

be any turning back. We have to get to the Great Hive, not just to make a new life there, but to warn the insects there. They have a very powerful, determined enemy. Queen Iriana won't stop till the Great Hive is destroyed."

Everything was silent for a moment as they took this in.

"I'm the only one who knows about the things that have yet to occur, and she knows it. I think she'll do anything to silence me." The group walked the tunnels in silence, stopping only when Celia checked the tunnel map drawn on the back of Anthony's map. Nobody knew how long they had been walking, but there were two things they did know: they had been walking for a *very* long time, and they had no plans of stopping.

After what seemed like an eternity, Celia said, "Finally! We're just about there. Maybe the bees that are supposed to live at the knoll can help us."

"Oh, I don't think we'll be getting any help," Anthony told her.

"Why not?"

"'Cause there's nobody here to give us help," Anthony answered as they entered. Sadly, he was right. Upon entering the beehive, they could all clearly see that it was devoid of even a single sign of life. It was deserted, empty, lifeless, and really creepy.

"Where did all the bees go?" Celia asked as she looked around.

"I think I have a pretty good idea," Anthony told Celia. Then they both heard Artie whimper. He sat sniffing what looked like the carcass of a dead bee. Or more accurately, a murdered bee. It lay slumped against the wall, with an axe lodged in its helmet.

"The hornets must have gotten here first," Celia concluded. "The entire hive smells like burnt honeycomb. At least we're the only ones here, though."

"We aren't alone, Celia."

"How are you sure?"

"Look!" Anthony whispered to Celia. He pointed to the third level of honeycomb, where worker bees would store honey for emergency rations. A gang of wasps and hornets sat around a small campfire, eating cooked maple leaves and talking quietly to each other. Anthony and Celia hid Tramonto, Alba, and Artie under a loose slab of rubble so that they could eavesdrop on the conversation.

"Well I say," declared a portly, spear-bearing wasp loudly, "that we cut our losses and shove off before anyone misses us, which no one probably will."

"Well, I'm *tellin'* you that we're stuck 'ere until *Her Majesty* begins the reconstruction. Till then, we six are stuck guarding the place."

"Ya shouldn't talk that way about Queen Iriana, Lloyd. She's gonna bring about a new era of greatness, she says. She makes a darn good point too: we've got power, so we ought to make good use of it." A few more nodded in agreement.

"These soldiers are so disillusioned," Celia whispered to Anthony.

"I know," Anthony agreed. "These are just some of the things I heard about. Iriana's says that she's going to 'colonize' the entire area, mostly by force. This beehive must've been her first stop."

Anthony and Celia were about to listen to more, but before Anthony was able stop him, Artie let off an ear-splitting howl. Back at the tunnel exit emerged twenty hornets, wasps, and rove beetles armed to the teeth (a figure of speech—they had none) with crossbows, swords, throwing daggers, even a poleax. Almost all were weapons of precision. There was an assassin bug among them, with a belt loaded with darts that he would spit out of his own mouth, which resembled an elephant's trunk.

"Looks like we have more company than we bargained for." Anthony laughed nervously. He scooped up the howling Artie, and he and Celia mounted their steeds.

"Luppolo!" they both cried in unison. Tramonto and Alba hopped away like the wind, the wasps and hornets following in their wake.

"C'mon, you bloated lummoxes!" Lieutenant Harquebus shouted to the guards on duty. "Give us a hand catching those fugitives!" The guards happily obliged, relieved to be free of their miserable post.

Meanwhile, Tramonto was facing some difficulties retaining speed, due to the quartz shard in his right hind leg. The arrows from the platoon's crossbows began to strike ever nearer to Anthony.

"Hurry up! They're gaining on us!" Celia shouted to Anthony.

"I can't. Tramonto's been wounded! We need to lose these guys," Anthony returned. "Let's try crisscrossing!" It was a risky trick, but it was definitely worth the risk. When Anthony veered Tramonto to the left, Celia would veer Alba to the right, and vice versa. The trick easily

evaded the hornets' projectiles, much to the frustration of the lieutenant.

"Faster, fly faster! Get in close quarters, and dice them up!" he snarled at his troops. "The price on their heads is big enough to keep you all fat and happy for the rest of your miserable lives!" At this, the troops sped up considerably, each enjoying his or her daydreams of fancy living. "Delilah, take their left! Rhea, take their right! You two pinch 'em and we'll gut 'em!'" Harquebus ordered. The two hornets, Delilah and Rhea, swooped down on both sides of Anthony and Celia. They used their spears like pokers, forcing the pair to cut their crisscrosses shorter and shorter in order to avoid being skewered. Soon Anthony and Celia were squashed together side by side, the hornet spear tips jabbing too close for comfort.

"Now, fall in!" Harquebus commanded. His troops fell from the air like lead weights, hovering just above the escaping ants. For the first time ever, Anthony raised his shield. The enemies' arrows and blows rattled off of its gleaming surface without leaving even a dent, while Celia used her backpack as an efficient substitute. An annoyed Harquebus fell upon Celia, hacking into her left top shoulder with his curved sword. His eyes shined with satisfaction as she clutched the injured arm with pain. Seeing his target unguarded, Harquebus took his opportunity to perform the finishing blow. But he was surprised to meet resistance from an enraged Anthony. As Anthony became locked in combat with the lieutenant as he leaned off of Tramonto with his sword drawn.

"Don't ever touch my friend!" he roared with each

strike. Harquebus was overwhelmed by Anthony's wild swings and finally fell back, ordering his platoon to follow suit. With the enemy out of sight, Anthony and Celia turned right into the next hall.

"Thanks, uh, for the help back there, Anthony," Celia thanked him.

"No problem. I'd do anything for a friend." Cutting the sentimental moment short, Harquebus's platoon burst out of the honeycomb on their right and rained down another hail of arrows.

"Don't they *ever* run out of ammo?" asked Celia in disbelief as they ducked away. She turned to look at Anthony. "Are you crazy?" Anthony was seated backward on Tramonto, fighting hornets with shield and sword. A rove beetle jumped off of a hornet's back and landed on top of Anthony, causing him to lose control of Tramonto.

"Anthony, we've reached the exit!" A gaping hole in the wall faced them, but they were unable to stop.

"It's times like this when I wish I could fly!" Anthony screamed as they fell down, down out of the hive.

Up a Creek with No Paddle

Anthony and Celia freefell out of the beehive and away from the hornets and wasps, as did Tramonto, Alba, and poor little Artie. They fell and fell, spiraling into what seemed like an endless abyss. And then they landed in a mound of dirt.

"Did any of them follow us?" Celia asked Anthony.

"No," Anthony replied with relief. "Except for this rove beetle."

"Is it conscious?"

Anthony battered it with his shield, and it collapsed. "Not anymore." The five stumbled out of the mound and looked up at the beehive from where they stood.

It was nestled in the branches of a lone squat sycamore fig that rested atop the rocky knoll. The knoll had earned its name from early human inhabitants who noticed the perpetual breezes that seemed to linger around it. Winding past the base of the knoll was Caris Creek, which traveled north into Bullfrog Bayou. It was just wide enough for a person to kayak on, which locals often did.

"Good," said Anthony. "We've found the creek, but we don't know how to travel it fast enough so that those worm brains back at the beehive won't catch us."

"I've got an idea. How about we don't waste our time thinking of travel when we could be traveling," suggested Celia. They mounted Tramonto and Alba and rode alongside the creek until they came upon a young palm tree. Around there it was hard for Anthony and Celia to hear each other over the spray of churning water from the creek.

"Look over here!" Anthony shouted. "I've found coconuts!"

"What?" Celia responded equally loudly. "You've gone loco and nuts?"

"No! *Coconuts*!" Anthony ran over to a pile of coconuts dropped from the palm tree, some fresh and some dried out.

"This is no time for a drink, Anthony! We need to get going!"

"I don't mean to *drink* out of them," Anthony explained. I mean to ride them."

"You're not making any sense right now."

"We could use this dried-out shell as a boat and go down the creek in it."

"All right, let's do it. But we'd better hurry, I can hear

the worm brains coming," Celia agreed, adopting the new nickname Anthony had invented for their pursuers. From where they were standing, they could hear the humming of the enemy in flight.

With some difficult rolling, they launched the shell and loaded Artie and their steeds onto it. With a kick from Anthony, their watercraft was soon being pulled downstream.

"Aw man, we should have remembered oars," Celia complained.

"Why's it such a big deal?" Anthony asked, too awed by the untamed force of the creek to care.

"Because *they* do have oars." Anthony looked backward and saw to his dismay that the search-and-destroy platoon had caught up with them. A group of rove beetles in canoes, along with the regular team of hornets and wasps, trailed them.

"Just try and catch us, worm brains!" Anthony taunted.

"Please don't goad them, Anthony," Celia warned. But it was too late. The platoon had launched into full pursuit. Lieutenant Harquebus leveled himself next to their boat.

"Anchor yourselves, fugitives. Or else your corpses will lie at the bottom of the creek before you reach the bayou!"

"Not before you do, hell-o jacket!" Anthony laughed.

"Insolent whelp! I'll have your guts for garters!"

"You wear garters?" Enraged, Harquebus took a swipe at Anthony's head. But Anthony was quicker and knocked the sword out of Harquebus's grasp with his own sword. Truly sick and tired of the wiseacre ant, Harquebus landed

in the coconut boat. No sooner had he landed, however, than Alba gave him a powerful kick out of the boat.

"Good girl," Celia praised the cricket. Harquebus pulled himself into the canoe of a chasing rove beetle.

"After that coconut!" he declared angrily. Those fugitives had insulted him far enough. The boats were entering rapids, at the part of the creek called the whitewater. The rove beetle propelling Harquebus's canoe was beginning to lose control.

"Gimme those oars!" he snarled, shoving the beetle out of the canoe. He easily took control of the craft, dodging past obstructing rocks that the other canoes crashed into, for he had eyes only for the ants. His aerial soldiers weren't having much luck with finding their mark. Even without any cover or shielding, the ants and their steeds in the coconut shell were well hidden by the spray of mist from the whitewater. "They're passing the rocks! Wait for them there and make pincushions out of them!"

"What rocks?" Anthony asked himself nervously. They were at the end of the creek, and above the spray he could see a wall of jagged rocks rise out of the water before the coconut boat, only a narrow opening visible between the rocks.

"Get ready to abandon ship!" Celia shouted. They mounted Tramonto and Alba as the rocks loomed nearer.

"Now!" Anthony and Celia kicked off from the coconut boat a split second before it slammed into the rocks along with the rove beetle canoes. However, they hadn't noticed the six-foot waterfall behind the rocks.

The waterlogged Lieutenant Harquebus had escaped his canoe just in time. The others had been crushed against the rocks. Behind those rocks was the waterfall, which emptied the creek into Bullfrog Bayou.

"Any sign of the ants?" Harquebus asked one of his wasps.

"None, sir," she answered. "They disappeared into the mist behind the waterfall. They left only their boat behind."

"Search the area surrounding the waterfall, every nook and cranny. Report to me when you've found them, or at least a clue as to where they are hiding." The wasp buzzed off to form the search party. Harquebus stared into the mossy bayou. He thought of the fugitive ant that had made a mockery of him. "Soon *I'll* be the one laughing, boy."

Bullfrog Bayou

Anthony, Celia, Artie, Tramonto, and Alba had put as much distance between themselves and the waterfall as they could. They found shelter for the evening in an empty rabbit warren. If they could have, they would have kept going, but they hadn't rested for two days straight. As the moon rose, Anthony and Celia sat warming their bodies around a campfire while drinking cups of Artie's sweet, acidic honeydew. Tramonto and Alba shared a leaf of wild lettuce to prepare for the final journey.

"I wish I had never told you what I heard in the duct," Anthony told Celia.

"How come?" Celia asked.

"I dragged us *both* into this mess. I've been in over my head ever since I eavesdropped on Iriana. Now we're like criminals or fugitives or something. If we don't get to the Great Hive, where will we hide?"

"You're being too hard on yourself, Anthony. I'm just as much a part of this as you are, and there's no other place I would rather be." She put her arm around Anthony comfortingly. "What are friends for, right?"

The next morning, after a long, long semi-sleep, Anthony and Celia woke up to the sight of a twitching pink nose poking inside the warren.

"That must be the rabbit that lives here," Celia said to Anthony. "I'll go talk to it. Maybe it can understand us." Celia crawled up the rabbit's side and onto its left ear. "Hey," she said into the rabbit's ear, "do you understand me?" The rabbit nodded. "Good, because I need your help. See that coconut shell?" Celia pointed to the waterfall. "My friend and I need you to push that into the water for us, and then we'll be on our way."

The rabbit scampered up the rocks beside the waterfall and nudged the coconut shell into the mossy water of the bayou. Anthony, Celia, and their three tired companions packed up and loaded onto their coconut boat. This time they brought oars of long grass that they had made the night before. Once they were in, their rabbit friend gave them a starting push.

"Thank you!" Anthony called back. The rabbit nodded in reply and crawled back into its warren.

"Such nice critters around here," Celia commented.

"Too bad the ones chasing us aren't so nice," Anthony

muttered. He worried about when Harquebus's platoon would find them. He didn't have to wait long. The telltale humming came from not far behind their boat, and Anthony and Celia heard an all-too-familiar voice ring out, "There they are!"

Lieutenant Harquebus and his troops swooped in for the kill as Anthony and Celia paddled for their lives from the sides of the shell. An arrow from Harquebus's crossbow sunk into the deck of the coconut boat, a hair away from Anthony's foot. None of those involved in the action noticed the water becoming murkier or the branches above becoming thicker as they carried on deeper into the bayou.

The tree roots that protruded from the muck blocked the way of the coconut boat, and they were forced to crawl out. Even on the backs of Tramonto and Alba, the two ants couldn't make up for the head start their pursuers had gained.

"It looks like we're goners now," Celia moaned grimly. Harquebus took an axe from a soldier's belt and raised it high above his head.

"I'm going to enjoy this, boy!"

"Aiiieeooww!" Artie let off a record-breaking howl. The melee ceased, and all heads turned toward the murk. Out of it emerged a pair of bulging eyes with oval pupils, atop a slimy head attached to a bloated body that undoubtedly belonged to the bayou's namesake: a bullfrog. It was an adult male, seven inches long, with its long hind legs ready to spring. Like the crack of a whip, the frog's tongue lashed out at Harquebus. And even quicker, Harquebus shoved one of his soldiers in the way, sacrificing him to

the bullfrog's slimy jaws. The bullfrog burped out the hornet's crumpled-up armor.

"*Run*!" Anthony screamed. Tramonto and Alba were all too happy to oblige, hopping away as fast as their legs cold carry them.

"Don't let them out of your sight!" Harquebus cried. His troops also were happy to get as far away as possible from the bullfrog. However, many other pairs of eyes rose out of the muck, and soon the water was churning with bullfrogs and tadpoles, all of them sensing the swarm of food buzzing just overhead. The amphibian army hopped over tree roots and swam under lilies after their retreating meal. Harquebus watched his troops get plucked out of the air by the slippery whips that were the frogs' tongues. Anthony and Celia hopped past pools of tadpoles that jumped out of the water to snap at them as they passed. The two just missed the jaws of a bullfrog as it lurched out of the mire.

"That was a close one," Anthony murmured as they sprang over the back of an emerging bullfrog. Celia saw the tops of two tadpoles' head tearing through the surface of the water like shark fins.

"Tadpoles at three o'clock!" Celia cried to Anthony. The rotted stick they were hopping across snapped, putting Tramonto and Alba in the position of thrashing their way to solid ground. Lieutenant Harquebus, who was not too far behind, seized this opportunity without hesitation. He swooped down to hack at Anthony with his axe, only to be driven back by a tide of tadpoles. Anthony and Celia had figured out that there was little solid ground in the

bayou, except for the roots of trees, and there was surely some sort of hungry amphibians under those.

A desperate bullfrog performed a spectacular leap out of the water, missing his intended targets entirely and capsizing Tramonto and Alba with an equally spectacular splash. Anthony, Celia, Tramonto, Alba, and Artie were pulled, gasping, underwater. They could see beneath the water the legions of bullfrogs and tadpoles chasing the scent of insect. *It's over*, Anthony thought. The trumpeting croaks grew louder. And then they all swam away. *Huh?* Suddenly the ground rose beneath them, and Anthony and Celia noticed the scaly, ridged hide they stood upon. In front of them, two scaly lumps rose out of the water.

"We're on an alligator!" Celia cried with relief. "We're saved!" The alligator snorted water out of its nostrils and swam off through the bayou.

"At this rate, we should reach Rindou Forest in no time at all," Anthony declared cheerfully. "Great Hive, here we come!"

Race through Rindou

Anthony, Celia, Artie, Tramonto, and Alba rested sleepily on the alligator's armored back. When they awoke, it was in the late afternoon and the setting sun set the clouds on fire as it disappeared from sight. The treetops high above them thinned out, and the murky bayou water and hammocks gave way to looming pine trees and forest.

"This must be Rindou," Anthony said to Celia. "Any sign of the worm brains?"

"Not so far," Celia reported. "And if there were, Artie would let us know." Artie squealed happily from Tramonto's saddle.

"Well then, it looks like smooth sailing from here on in."

Lieutenant Harquebus sat in a pine tree with ten of his former twenty-five soldiers, licking his wounds.

"Stupid bayou," he muttered sulkily. "Stupid tadpoles, stupid bullfrogs, stupid fugitives. How could I let those ants escape *again*?" Harquebus sniveled. The ant boy's laughing still rang in his ears, mocking him, goading him. He pulled himself together. "Well, they've crossed the wrong yellowjacket. Troops, ready your weapons, and let's get moving! If we don't have those ants' heads before they reach the Great Hive, then Queen Iriana will have ours!"

Iriana was indeed in a nasty mood. As she hovered down the fungus caverns to her sister's oubliette, she thought of how that yellowjacket, Harquebus, had not contacted her in days. *Has he caught them yet, I wonder*? Iriana dropped through the trapdoor-style entrance to her sister's holding cell. Her sister sat waiting for her. *This is odd*, Iriana thought. *She seems... healthier*. She drew the vial of the noxious potion out of her crown. "It's time again, sister."

"Very well." Vespa was unusually calm. When she let the potion slide down her throat, however, she collapsed in disgust.

"You can't fool me, sister," Iriana laughed. "I knew you were developing immunity to the potion, so I added an extra ingredient. Just a bit of scorpion's venom, not quite enough to kill you."

"Why do you bother keeping me alive anyway?" Vespa questioned Iriana.

"I want you alive long enough to witness my conquest of all the terrain before me. I don't want you to die before the kingdom that forgot you becomes the greatest empire in Interra, maybe even *the world*." Vespa shook her head. There was once a time when she believed that Iriana was insane. But she was wrong. Now she knew that her sister was a complete psychopath!

Anthony and Celia galloped toward the Great Hive with excitement in their small insect hearts. They were almost there, alive and in one piece. Or at least that's what they thought. At that moment Lieutenant Harquebus arrived with his remaining troops, maddened with desperation.

"Don't hold back. Do not hesitate! *They must not reach the hive*!" Harquebus shouted. Their arrows swooped down on the two ants like a flock of ravens.

"We've gotten this far," Anthony shouted to Celia, "and these worm brains aren't going to stop us now!" Harquebus dropped from the air and swung his axe at Anthony's head.

"When I am through with you," Harquebus barked, "Her Majesty will reward me for you and your friend's death with two hundred trins, and her daughters will share in eating your remains!"

"The only thing *you're* going to be eating is our dust!" Celia retorted. In his anger, Harquebus swung his axe and hacked off Alba's left foot. She continued to move, hob-

bling over the ground, her jumps not covering as much distance. One of the assassin bug's darts whizzed past Celia's antennae, another sinking into her backpack.

"*This'll teach you both not to laugh at me*!" Harquebus screamed, frothing at the mouth. As he brought his axe down, Anthony chucked Artie from Tramonto's saddle. The half-inch aphid clung resolutely to Harquebus's head, biting him all the while. "Aarrgh! Get'm off of me!"

"Hop on to Tramonto!" Anthony told Celia. "Alba will be able to hop faster if she doesn't have to carry your weight!"

"What about my weight?" Celia asked, offended.

"Just get on!" Celia threw herself from Alba's saddle and settled herself behind Anthony's abdomen. One wasp above them tossed a quartz cluster that detonated upon impact with the forest floor. A cloud of steam and soil was tossed up, and Anthony raised his shield to protect them from the flying quartz shards. And out of the veil of debris they saw it—the Great Hive—in all of its honeycomb-like glory.

The aboveground structure stood twenty-five feet high, a yellowish dome, and there was even more belowground.

"We're here!" Anthony and Celia cried in unison. But Lieutenant Harquebus refused to see his quarry escape so easily. After tearing Artie off of his face, he zipped up the bulging brown sack that held the platoon's quartz clusters. He inserted a lit match into the corner of the zipper. Anthony saw the lit projectile coming as he caught Artie. As the improvised bomb and the hornets approached, a sun-eclipsing hail of arrows came to meet them.

Lieutenant Harquebus cared nothing for the slaughter of his troops by the arrows coming from the top of the Great Hive. His eyes were locked on the two ants and their steeds that were catapulted into the air by his explosive. Harquebus's eyes shined at the idea that he might at last be rid of the fugitives. But when he looked through the glowing blaze, he saw no trace of them.

"*No, no, no, no*!" Harquebus spat and sobbed and pounded the ground. He had failed. The ants had reached the Great Hive.

Part Three: War of the Hives

The Hive at Last

"'They shall not live to see the hive.' Were those not your exact words, Lieutenant Harquebus? Or should I say *ex-lieutenant*?" Harquebus trembled with fright as his infuriated queen loomed over him.

"I assure you, my queen," plead Harquebus, attempting to calm her, "the fugitives' resourcefulness was underestimated."

"Oh, I underestimated them, did I?" Iriana thrust Harquebus against the walls of her quarters. "Well, perhaps I overestimated you. The general held you in very high esteem, but I intend to make an example of your true character."

"What are you going to do?" Harquebus eked out.

"You will be demoted, ostracized, rejected, beaten, lashed, and branded. You'll receive one thousand lashes for your undependability!" Iriana wrenched a steaming torch

from the wall and thrashed Harquebus across his back. She chased him out, beating him and screaming, "If I am able to conjure a punishment, you will experience it! Get out, out, out, you miserable slug! Don't bother showing your unworthy hide in my presence again, understand? Get out, you worthless maggot!" She flew to the top of the massive oak that was her kingdom. She glared at the Great Hive with madness burning in her eyes. "This means *war*!"

Thousands of insects gathered around the sturdy main-gate entrance to the Great Hive, crowding the two unconscious arrivals.

"They're coming to!" one insect cried. The two ants, their steeds, and one aphid moaned as they painfully regained consciousness.

"Thank Agoz," Anthony gasped in wonder. "Celia, look!" Celia awoke grumpily to find herself within the magnificent dome.

"Wow," was all she could manage. For once in her ant life she was speechless. Artie sniffed the new scents around him with excitement.

"Out of my way, move along, coming through!" Anthony frowned when he saw Hawthorne, the grumpy horsefly, come shoving through the thick crowd. He noticed Anthony immediately. "You're here, but how?"

"Anthony, Celia!" Gregorak, the goliath beetle, lifted them inches off the ground in a cheerful hug. "I'm glad to see that you both made it here in one piece. Well, almost one piece. You surely both have quite a story to tell."

"You have no idea." Anthony laughed.

"Ah, so we meet again, young ant." The crowd parted respectfully as the huge bright-green Chinese mantis from Anthony's vision approached the two to greet them. "And you have brought friends. It is not every day that we welcome guests who arrive with such a bang." The mantis stretched his mouth sections in a smile, although it dissolved a moment later. "I sense that your journey was not without its perils. You may tell me what has passed during tonight's banquet."

"Banquet?" Celia asked hungrily.

"Indeed, it is a pre-festival tradition here, which I invite you to join us in. But for now, Gregorak will show you to your rooms." The goliath beetle took Anthony, Celia, and Artie in his arms and flew them to the sixth level above them and deposited them in front of the door to a room that resembled a hotel room.

"You'll sleep on this level during your stay here," Gregorak told Anthony. "The feast banquet will begin shortly. I'll see you there." He beckoned Celia. "Your room is at the other side of the Great Hive, so this might be a long flight." Gregorak and Celia waved good-bye to Anthony and Artie. After Gregorak showed Celia to her room, Hawthorne flew over.

"I suspect those kids," he grumbled. "You saw the explosion when they arrived here. Mu-Ra might be treating them like heroes, but I'm not convinced. They've both brought doom to us all, I'm sure of it."

"You must have faith, friend," Gregorak sighed. "It's

not wise to make such early conclusions about newcomers. And I can't easily recall a time that Mu-Ra was wrong about an insect."

As Gregorak hummed away on his powerful shelled wings, Hawthorne muttered to himself, "That boy'll be the death of us all, and that beady-eyed beetle isn't gonna convince me otherwise."

Anthony and Celia sat at the main table in the Hive cafeteria. Anthony sat at Mu-Ra's right, and Celia sat at his left. The fifteen-foot-long main table was decorated with decadent and delicious delicacies. Tender meats, tropical fruits, fresh vegetables, flower blossoms, cheeses, honeydew, grasshopper beef, succulent seafood, and even pastries for dessert; all was prepared by the Great Hive's master chefs, who followed recipes passed down from human to animal and then to insect. Mu-Ra whistled into a reed megaphone to gather everyone's attention; the cafeteria was made for sound to echo.

"Champions, knights, and dwellers of our hallowed hive," the mantis began, "tonight we host two honored guests, who have a great deal to tell me and the rest of the Great Hive. Their names are Anthony and Celia, and these two ants have traveled from miles afar with the intention of being accepted into the ranks of champions. It is my wish that our population welcome them as friends and family. On that pleasant note, let the banquet begin!" The insects cheered and dug in. Anthony selected a grasshopper thigh, a glass of 1894 Trellis white wine (which

Mrs. Daemond would've *never* allowed him to drink), and a slice of lemon. Celia had a slice of celery coated in peanut butter and a glass of warm spring water.

"Best food ever," Anthony declared with a full mouth.

"I couldn't agree more," Celia agreed, licking excess peanut butter off of her face. Every insect within the Great Hive was enjoying the sumptuous feast equally; Gregorak had a whole grasshopper leg, and Mu-Ra ate an entire grasshopper. Artie joined other aphids in a head of lettuce. Then there came dessert, during which Anthony and Celia drifted away into chocolate heaven. Mu-Ra dismissed them with a quick prayer.

"May In shine brightly upon us," he prayed, using the name of the mother of all insects and the insect gods and goddesses. The attendees walked away with full stomachs and sleepy heads. "Tell me," Mu-Ra asked the two bloated ants as they struggled up the grand spiral staircase to the third floor, "what did you discover during your journey?" When they were sure that none were paying attention, Anthony and Celia climbed up Mu-Ra's narrow upper body and whispered into his ear hole the events that had passed during their trek there. The mantis's antennae twitched with distaste as Anthony described Iriana's diabolical plans.

"This news is somewhat unsurprising to me," Mu-Ra said. "No activity has been seen from the Zephyr's Knoll beehive for days. And to think that Regius City has fallen." Mu-Ra shook his head. "It is to our disadvantage that we cannot declare outright war."

"Why can't we?" Celia asked.

"If what Anthony says is correct, then Iriana has been

gaining territory all around us. Termite mounds, anthills, beehives—all are being found desolate, and the scouts we send to investigate rarely return. It's quite ironic how such dismal events should precede such a joyous celebration."

"The Moon Festival?" Anthony asked hopefully. "We haven't missed it?"

"Indeed not." Mu-Ra laughed. "Perhaps you lost track of time on your journey. The Moon Festival doesn't begin for four days, on June the twenty-ninth." Anthony finally reached his room. "I sense an aura of inspiration about you, Anthony," Mu-Ra told him. "If you and Celia still wish, you may become a Hive pupil."

"We do!" Anthony and Celia cried in unison. The mantis smiled. He had expected such an enigmatic response.

"Your tutelage shall begin immediately," Mu-Ra told them. Though mostly the entire Great Hive slept that night (all except for the nocturnal insects), Anthony and Celia were kept awake with excitement and most of all, hope.

Iriana's Monologue

In the cathedral of the Hive of Vesthrax, Father Antistes, the same wasp priest who delivered Queen Vespa the First's eulogy, sat alone in the steeple, the tip of the knot on the oak tree's branch that formed the cathedral. The gaps in the spacious knot had been sealed with beautiful stained glass. It had been a long day of confessions for Antistes; wasps and hornets alike had weaved sorrowful tales of starvation, theft, neglect, and bereavement.

Iriana had decreed that 60 percent of food scavenged by scouts would be shipped to the soldiers serving in the conquer campaign and that the rest be rationed for the hive dwellers. Since then, many families, even some of Iriana's unclaimed daughters (only queen larvae are claimed as official daughters of the queen) had been left to starve. Iriana had assured her subjects that food supplies

would return to normal and that the lack of acceptance of her regime by the colonized provinces and independent societies was to blame. She also claimed that the only reason for forceful colonization was to prevent early backlash from the colonized territories.

"Such sorrow has spawned from Her Majesty's lust for conquest," Father Antistes sighed, "yet the cries of the people have still been stifled by her blatant injustice."

"You always were the drama queen, Antistes." The aged wasp spun around to see Iriana casually reclined on the windowsill behind him. "Truly depressing confessions, those were," she admitted. "Starvation, death, misery; but it will heal, I'm sure."

"When, Your Majesty?" Father Antistes pleaded. "When can we end this accursed campaign? When will you listen to reason?"

"Interestingly enough," Iriana continued, ignoring Antistes, "was the mention of the next ration shipment. I hadn't heard any news of the date; why it was almost as if you had some part in organizing it."

Father Antistes, knowing this would end very painfully for him, dove for the opposite window. Iriana grabbed his left wing and forced him to the ground. "Now it's time for a little confessing on *your part*," Iriana hissed, kicking Antistes cruelly in the backside. "As a highly respected member of our hive parish, you're the last insect I'd expect to be stealing rations behind my back. Our honored Father Antistes, a common thief? What would the hive dwellers think?"

"Most already know." This took Iriana aback.

"I knew it!" She dragged Antistes by one wing and

directed him down the steps of the steeple. When they were in the bottom level of the church, Iriana threw him to the floor once again and shoved a lit candle in front of the quivering wasp's face.

"Why, Your Highness? Why? What wrought this demon's curse upon you?" Antistes lay with his both pairs of legs and his abdomen curled into fetal position, as if he were already dead.

"Oh, *cram it*, Father," Iriana spat. But her mind was somewhere else, dragged into her subconscious by the priest's question. Memories floated around her like teardrops suspended in mid-fall; to her that's exactly what they were: the chronicles of the many tears shed in her childhood. She could hardly hear herself reciting the hardships of her early life to Father Antistes.

"It didn't start when I was a larva. I was just another claimed queen larva, my unclaimed sisters catering to my every whim along with the other claimed sisters, including the early Vespa the Second. After years of eating and growing, the time to spin our cocoons came. I was one of the last to emerge as a full-grown hornet, and it was something that I carried with me into my later childhood.

"My sisters were unyielding in their taunt about 'sister last hatched' for most of those precious remaining years before true royal responsibility. So I sulked in my spare time away from my sisters and wandered alone throughout the surrounding Rindou Forest. Those hours of loneliness were treasured hours, an escape from my humiliation, for it wasn't only my cruel sisters who degraded me, oh no. There were the jealous senior hornets and wasps that

claimed to my mother, 'She's unfit for the responsibility of the crown. Her late metamorphosis and obvious frailty is an undeniable sign of weakness.' Those words to my mother crushed me. News spread across the whole bloody oak that I might be denied the crown if I inherited it. So I ran away from the responsibility I would never have had, only to stumble across an unforeseen one. I found an ant's egg, just lying there in the forest, amid the tracks of an anteater. That egg was the cure to my emptiness, something to care for, to nurture. So I returned home and cared for it in secrecy until it hatched into a young female slavemaker ant. Even though I was young, she was like a daughter to me. Little did I know that her real mother was queen of a slavemaker ant colony, based on an anteater-mounted fortress. For caring for her daughter in her absence, her entire colony honored me, and I soon had very powerful allies.

"But when that beloved little ant died, the queen died of a broken heart, and they were devastated. Who did they have to guide them? Nobody, save for me. I was a hornet acting as a queen of a colony of nomadic ants; I had power that my foolish sisters had not yet inherited. The slavemakers taught me things, things that were terrible and great. I learned the exotic and arcane practices of their homeland. They taught me basic alchemy—how to make a potion that a plant can absorb to makes its surface flammable and how to concoct a noxious poison that can cripple a victim yet suspend him or her in life.

"When I saw my own sisters frolicking among the forest bushes, the opportunity for revenge overwhelmed me,

blinded me, and *consumed me*. The anteater plucked them from the branches; trying to sting its tongue did nothing to help them. Conveniently enough, dear sister Vespa was not present to be devoured. When the news reached home, my mother, my sister, *the whole hive* was devastated, and I felt a disgusting guilt only the vilest criminals should ever feel.

"When sister came to me for comfort, weeping her remorse to me, I could hear none of her words, only her past taunts. I gave her the crippling potion, telling her it would make everything better, and it did... well, at least for me. I dragged her deep under the roots of the oak tree, into a hidden oubliette, which Mother had once said was reserved only for the most heinous criminals. I felt like throwing myself in there for a time. When the pain healed, only Mother was left to hold the crown, and when she confessed her love for me, I realized that her apologies didn't quench my thirst for vengeance. So I killed her—I beat her over the head with her own crown and tossed her body into Bullfrog Bayou. I left a weighted dummy to be found and buried.

"Since I had no one left, I flew to the Great Hive, and for over a year I accepted their tutelage. The mantis said I could have been great; that is, had they not found that an entire slavemaker ant colony had pledged its allegiance to me. They shunned me without trial; they cast me out and banished me. I learned from those tumultuous events that even when the things you care for are destroyed, what you gain from the aftermath, the power you reap from the shards of a shattered love, are the things that really matter. And when you can return to a place that spurned you, enslaving

it and its idiot inhabitants is the only way to forgive their sins. The only solace they can offer is their fealty."

Father Antistes was petrified. *I presided over the coronation of a monster! The hive that was once home to the goddess of wasps and hornets, the only hive to house both cousin species, it is ruined*! The solemn queen gazed down at him with distaste. She had no use for him any longer, and she shoved the still-burning candle into his face. While his screams of pain were still muffled by the melting wax, Iriana threw him out of the closest stained-glass window. "I have said too much," she realized. She flew out of the cathedral, hoping no one had witnessed the heinous event that had taken place.

A Hard Day's Work

It was a beautiful sun-filled morning, and Anthony was shoveling cricket droppings in the Great Hive stables with his new friend, Alleo Fond, a bumblebee.

"Is it true what everyone is saying," he asked Anthony incredulously.

"What would that be?" Anthony questioned back.

"That you were chased here by hornets and wasps and rove beetles."

"It's all as true as I'm covered in cricket crap."

Anthony laughed and shoveled another pile into the hole.

"You know, the life of a hive pupil isn't all guts and glory," Alleo explained. "It's also about self-sacrifice and enlightenment."

"You've been listening to Mu-Ra again, haven't you?"

"Unfortunately, yes." They both laughed together.

"Let me guess," Anthony said sarcastically, "it only gets better from here, right?"

"Actually, it does. Believe me, we won't be shoveling Nightshade's droppings forever." Nightshade was the crabby male cave cricket that belonged to Hawthorne. The boys working in the stables had nicknamed him "Deadly Nightshade" because he was as bad tempered as his master. Anthony learned this the hard way when a kick from the cricket's long legs had sent him tumbling into the smelly pile of his droppings. Nightshade made a hiss that sounded suspiciously like a chuckle.

"Oh, you think that's funny?" Anthony asked, losing his temper. "Well, I bet you won't think it's so funny when I take this shovel and shove it up your—"

"What's all this shouting?" an irritable voice asked.

"Nice going, Anthony," Alleo sighed.

"What are you, some sort of dung beetle larva?" Hawthorne mocked Anthony. This comment denoted an enormous amount of insensitivity, for there were many dung beetles at the Great Hive, and some already endured enough taunts from outsiders. "Now, quit wallowing in filth and get shoveling. And I had *better not* see any bruises on that cricket!" The horsefly flew out of the stables, still grumbling.

"Yes, sir," Anthony muttered under his breath.

"I feel your pain, man," Alleo said. Anthony didn't respond. *I wonder if Celia is having as much* fun *as I am,* Anthony thought.

Celia was actually having quite a bit of fun. She was becoming very efficient with the short curved sword she had filched from Harquebus. Her mentor was a quirky, hilarious Mexican American mosquito named Guido.

"C'mon, girl, you think you can take on a hornet at *your* snail's pace? Bind. That's it, left, *left*. Of course, I attacked your right, duh! It's called a feint. Aye carumba, senorita, you're a real killer with that blade of yours, eh?"

Celia was doubled over with laughter by the time Guido was done with his jabbering. They both sheathed their swords. "So," Guido asked, "are you and that Anthony an item yet?"

"What?" Celia questioned.

"Oh, nothing," defended Guido, playing innocent. "I just couldn't help noticing that you two were oddly close, ya know? Two ants in puberty on a long journey; it seems to me like the sort of thing that would bring two love bugs together."

"Guido!" The mosquito laughed as Celia jokingly punched him on the arms.

"We're just good friends," Celia explained. "We met when we were practically larvae, and it's been that way ever since. But we're just friends, got it?"

"Whatever you say, senorita, *whatever* you say." The mosquito pulled a canteen of flower nectar, a male mosquito's favorite drink, out of his saber belt and guzzled it down. "You know," Guido remembered, "the Great Hive has a huge library in the underground section, and I mean *huge*. You should really go check it out."

"A library?" Celia asked in wonder. Visiting a real library was something she had always dreamed of but could never do because her old colony couldn't afford one.

"Aye, and I believe you'll find the books there both helpful and amusing. And since you're blocking out everything I say right now, I'll leave you to your thoughts, senorita." Guido flew out of the training room, and Celia departed for the Great Hive Library.

Anthony and Alleo, newly washed up after shoveling the hated Nightshade's droppings, were summoned to the Great Hive library by an ecstatic Celia.

"You've got to come see this," Celia gasped, finding it hard to breathe.

"What's the big deal?" Anthony asked. "It's just a library."

Celia thought for a moment that her spiracles were clogged. "*Just* a library?" Celia repeated in disbelief. "This library is huge! Just wait till you see it!" Celia led the two bored friends through wooden doors and into the twists, turns, and maze-like aisles of the Great Hive library.

"Whoa." Neither Anthony nor Alleo could believe his eyes. The Great Hive library was one of the greatest achievements of insects in history; it was an astounding feat. The collection of different-sized texts rivaled that of any major human library.

"This is awesome," said Anthony. "They have books on practically *everything* here. Archery, sword fighting, history, royalty, kingdoms, empires, even how to make honey."

Anthony sat down in a comfortable couch with Alleo

and Celia and a book entitled *The History, Founding, and Construction of the Great Hive*. Celia chose a thick mantis-written tome called *Former and Current Kingdoms and Empires of Southeastern Interra,* and Alleo flipped through *Know Your Foe: the Anatomies and Strategies of a Plethora of Insects*.

After receiving a library membership from an elderly mantis librarian, the three left with their chosen books, eager to learn more.

"I'm learning a lot about the history of our enemies," Celia told Anthony back at his room. It was their precious time off from duties, training, or classes. Celia flipped to page 416. At the top of the page was the heading of a new section, which read, "The Hive of Vesthrax." She cleared her spiracle air passages—"*Ahem*"—and began reading.

"The Hive of Vesthrax is fabled as once having hosted the goddess of hornets and wasps, Vesthrax, thereby being named after her. It is the only hive in the world to host both species. The Hive of Vesthrax has also hosted a long line of great queens and commands a much-feared army, renowned for its ferocity, strategy, and size. The hive itself, however, technically isn't a hive. It is actually eight large hives housed within a massive oak tree. The hive's history also includes major political scandals, the most recently recorded being the sudden death of all of Queen Vespa the First's claimed daughters, with the exception of one."

Anthony and Alleo took this new information in slowly.

"Did you ask the librarian who the current queen was?" Alleo asked Celia.

"Yes," Celia answered grimly. "She said that their new ruler, Queen Iriana, has severed all contact with the Great Hive."

For a second, Anthony's small ant heart stopped.

"When the fighting starts," Anthony predicted, "we won't be outnumbered, but we'll be in for a ride." Anthony was interrupted by a knock at the door. Gregorak poked his head in.

"The Hive council wishes to see you two," he said. "Sorry, Alleo, but this is kind of private."

"I understand," Alleo replied. He waved good-bye to Anthony and Celia and buzzed out the door.

"Now, follow me," Gregorak told the two ants.

Anthony and Celia were led by Gregorak to a large room far across from the main entrance. Seated at a long table was the Great Hive council: Mu-Ra, Hawthorne, Guido, Angela, the Jamaican pill bug, Jessie, the Australian bulldog ant, and Flo, the lacewing fly.

"The council has been deliberating the decision of how to respond to further hostilities from Iriana's forces," Mu-Ra said. "We've decided that if she declares open warfare upon us, we will accept her challenge."

"*What*?" The protest came from Mu-Ra's far right, from Hawthorne. "Sending the Hive into open warfare on the word of two obnoxious ants?" Hawthorne protested further. "This is insane."

"*Have a seat, Hawthorne*," Mu-Ra ordered with some annoyance. The furious horsefly swore and muttered to himself.

"Ah, take a chill pill," Guido told Hawthorne.

"You have given us a great deal of valuable information," Mu-Ra continued. "My foreseeing ability can only tell me so much. It is thanks to you two that we have identified the Hive's hidden enemy."

"We owe you younguns a debt of gratitude," Jessie agreed.

"We would also appreciate it," Mu-Ra added, "if you would describe to us the extent of the damage dealt to the beehive on Zephyr's Knoll."

Anthony and Celia launched into the disturbing details of the beehive's state of decay, taking turns elaborating on the honeycomb rotted from days of neglect, littered corpses and larvae, and collapsed honey-making machinery.

"This is a disgrace," Mu-Ra sighed. "To raid is one thing, but to carelessly destroy? Intolerable. I thank you two for informing us. You are dismissed."

Artie's Misadventure

Meanwhile, Artie lounged happily on Anthony's bed, waiting patiently for his owner and best friend to return. He had visited Tramonto and Alba in the Great Hive's stables, and both were equally curious as to where the two ants were. After what seemed like an impossibly long period of waiting, Artie left Anthony's room.

Where could he be? Artie wondered. He zigzagged down the grand spiral staircase, shoving and nudging through bustling crowds of insects traveling up and down through the Hive's many levels.

"Hey, watch it!" one insect shouted as Artie nearly tripped him.

Why don't you *watch it*? Artie thought to himself. When he reached the ground floor, he had no clue where to look next. The Great Hive had a circumference of thirty meters

(over ninety-five feet), and Artie couldn't cover all of that ground. Then he caught a familiar scent.

Tunnels! *Anthony like tunnels*! Artie thought happily. He quickly dashed under several signs reading, "Do Not Enter! Tunneling Project Up Ahead; Authorized Entry Only." Artie continued into the spacious tunnel system, scanning the dirt and stone for any traces of Anthony or Celia's scent.

But after running and sniffing for an hour, Artie began to lose hope of finding his friends.

Come on, where are you guys? Artie wondered. He had traveled one mile away from the Great Hive and still had found no signs of the two ants, when he finally heard voices.

"Tunneling length at approximately three miles, sir," one voice said.

"Excellent. At this rate we'll reach our destination during the Moon Festival," the other answered. Artie recognized the nasally dirt-muffled grumbling as the voices of weevils.

They shouldn't give me any trouble, Artie thought. *Ninety-something percent of weevils don't reach over half of an inch.* But the foreman weevil that Artie saw was different.

His name was Ignatius Bugiardo, and he had a height (or if on six legs, length) of eight tenths of an inch. Much to his annoyance, hive dwellers insisted on calling him "Iggy," usually just for the sake of bugging him. The rest of Iggy's weevil workforce members were only about one half of an inch.

"We've been working on this project for years and years," Iggy sighed, "and now the reward will be ours." He gazed proudly at the gap his team had gouged into the dirt and rock. The tunnel must've continued for at least

three miles. "We'll be rich for this, boys, filthy, stinking rich." The weevils shook with a chorus of laughter that echoed eerily down the miles-long tunnel. Artie made to scramble back to the Great Hive and accidentally kicked dirt into an open lantern. The hiss of the dying flame caught the weevils' attention, and they had the aphid surrounded in the blink of an eye.

A rotund weevil digger lunged at Artie, who bit him on the arm. The strength of Artie's small-but-powerful jaws snapped off the weevil's tarsi, the end sections of an insect's arm, which acts as a fist for holding and handling objects. "Let's kill it!" one weevil shouted. The rest jumped into the fray with the agitated Artie, kicking, biting, shoving, and throwing cheap shots. One threw dirt in his eyes while another kicked him from behind. Then a weevil tugged on one antenna while a second weevil punched him in the side. Artie knew when he was fighting with cowards, and there was no doubt about it, those creeps were bona fide yellowbellies, every last one of them.

"Break it up, break it up! Out of the way, nimrods!" Ignatius shouted as he pushed through the mob. Seeing Ignatius, Artie snapped at his belt instinctively. Ignatius grabbed Artie with four arms, for he was a beetle that stood on two legs, and began squeezing his abdomen.

"Slippery little pest," Ignatius complained as Artie struggled, "just hold still, and it'll only hurt for *one second*."

Knowing full well where this was going, Artie blinded the weevil with a spray of honeydew. As fast as he could, Artie took off down the mile-long stretch of tunnel back to the Great Hive. When some of the weevils began to give chase, Ignatius called, "Let the aphid run. Tell the tunnel entrance lookouts to increase security. I've no doubt they were sleeping on the job again. But don't worry. The aphid doesn't know anything."

Quagmire Quarry

"Just another step, Anthony," Ben the centipede called down from the edge of the sandstone quarry. Alleo waited on a small cliff below Anthony to catch him in case he fell.

Quagmire Quarry used to be a popularly mined sandstone quarry, until the modern focus on recyclable metals left it abandoned. It was just northwest of the Great Hive, and to the east of the quarry was the stone viaduct that crossed over the valley that housed the Clover Fields Kingdom, ruled by the chieftains of the Clover cicada tribes. "I dunno, Ben," Alleo complained, "this place is safer for smaller insects."

"Why is that?" Anthony asked nervously.

"*That's* why," Ben answered, pointing down the quarry with many of his left arms. Anthony looked down to see the mottled brown and green hides of anoles and skinks that were crawling in and out of niches in the sandstone. The leg of a cockroach stuck out of the corner of one skink's mouth, and a green anole was still chowing down on an unfortunate moth.

"If you were a smaller insect, then the lizards and other predators would be less likely to prey on you," Alleo explained to the noticeably pale Anthony. "Just don't do *anything* to draw their attention." The boys had decided to come to the quarry while on their herding duty, which involved riding, flying, and running around the livestock pasture to herd the hoppers grazing there. Tramonto stood simpering at the edge of the quarry.

"Don't worry, boy," Anthony assured his grasshopper steed. "We're just going to a sunny spot to relax. I'll be back in just a sec." *Just stay unnoticed*, Anthony thought. *How hard can that be*?

"One pull of the trigger is all it takes," General Razorwing whispered to himself as he aimed at Anthony from his high perch in the quarry.

"Hold your fire, General." Iriana hovered in out of nowhere.

"You know, I hate it when you sneak up on me like that," the general sighed.

"Aim upward a bit more," she commanded, ignoring his complaint. He tilted the crossbow up just a little, aiming over Anthony's head.

"But if the bolt misses, they'll notice us," General Razorwing said.

"Maybe so," Iriana admitted, "but the lizards will notice them first."

Thwang! Anthony, Alleo, and Ben fell to the ground at the sound of a projectile being fired at them. The bolt clattered noisily to the bottom of the quarry, beaming an anole along the way. The annoyed reptile and several other bystanders looked up at the three fairly-healthy sized insects that they believed to have disturbed their peace.

Anthony looked over at Alleo and Ben, who were staring in horror at the many hungry reptiles advancing up the wall of the quarry.

"Oh, cricket crap."

Celia, meanwhile, was riding into the northwest pastures on Alba to check up on the boys. That was when she heard their screaming.

"Celia, *run away*!" Anthony hollered as he galloped toward her on the equally distressed Tramonto. Without so much as warning her, Anthony swung Celia onto Tramonto's saddle by the arm and continued hopping away.

"Anthony, what's the big rush?" Celia asked.

"Look behind me," Anthony answered without turning back.

"It can't be that b—*What did you do*?" Celia shouted, seeing the lizards scurrying after them.

"Well, it wasn't *me*, really," Anthony explained. "Someone ambushed us, and the attack startled the lizards." Tramonto jumped over the pasture fence into the pasture where the Great Hive's livestock was grazing. The lizards jumped over after them.

"They want the livestock!" The situation dawned on Celia. She turned to Anthony. "You idiot! You led them to our food!" She was right, of course.

The first lizard to come over the fence lost interest in Anthony completely and snapped up a nearby cricket. Emboldened by the success of a fellow reptile, the others followed suit. The livestock were helpless to avoid the attack. At the rate the lizards were munching, the Great Hive would probably starve for weeks.

"Send a distress signal!" Celia urged Anthony. "We can't handle this situation ourselves."

"But then everyone will know I started this," Anthony argued. "Most of the Hive is already suspicious about us. I won't give them any more reason to suspect us."

Celia had heard enough. If Anthony wasn't going to take action, then *she* was. Celia launched the Great Hive distress signal, a red box kite that all Hive dwellers had to carry while outside. Sentries would spot it and summon assistance immediately.

"What're you doing?" Anthony cried.

"We can worry about that headache of a horsefly later," Celia said to Anthony.

"Focus on the current situation, got it, hero boy?" Anthony smiled and nodded. Meanwhile, the livestock devastation continued. Think shark-feeding frenzies are violent? Ha! Even a crawling Gila monster lumbered into the pasture, crunching prey in time with its footsteps.

"Here they come." Celia pointed out the backup that was arriving. Hawthorne rode in on Nightshade, leading a team of other mounted hive dwellers.

"I knew it! I knew it!" Hawthorne shouted, yanking Anthony by the arm. "You can't worm your way out of this one, boy! I knew you were trouble, and now everyone else knows it!" Anthony felt the instinctive urge to punch the horsefly right in his smug mouth, but Celia stepped in, denying him his target.

"Lizards. Eating. Our. Food. How much clearer can I make it for you?" Celia said with annoyance. Without another response, Hawthorne and the others rode in against the lizards. This was Anthony's second time seeing the champions in action, and they did not disappoint.

There was Nightshade, biting the back of an anole while Hawthorne dug into its brow with his sword and his mandibles. Another's blade rattled off the teeth of a slithering, biting skink. Guido was showing off with his rapier—left, right, jab, jab! Each twirl of his blade meant another gash on the face for some unlucky lizard.

All of this action served as gladiatorial entertainment for one gleeful bystander.

"I *do* love this carnage." Iriana giggled, lounging on a sandstone cliff. "It really warms my heart to see all the efforts of those *brave* insects wasted as they're being dined upon by lizards. I only hope they save some Hive-dwellers for me, though."

"Any…bright…ideas?" Anthony asked Celia in between parries of lizard teeth. But he wasn't being sarcastic; their situation was desperate, and they had no game plan.

"I…I've got nothing," Celia admitted from the safety of an anthill bunker (the insect equivalent of a foxhole).

"I do." Alleo shoved Anthony into the anthill bunker and then climbed in himself. "Sniff my pollen pouch."

Anthony and Celia's antennae curled in disgust at the smell of the substance Alleo held in his pollen pouch.

"*Gross,*" Anthony said. "What's *in* there?"

"Pheromones," Alleo answered. "I hear it's lizard mating season."

Iriana was still watching the devastation with cruel intent, relishing every anguished squeal from the hive defenders. For her it was great fun, until it stopped.

Why are they turning back? she wondered as the lizards retreated. Then she realized that they weren't retreating; they were chasing her soldiers, about twenty of them, captured from their guarding post ten feet below her. The frightened wasps and hornets had been stripped of their wings and were forced to stumble down the quarry, with a legion of lizards in fevered pursuit.

Iriana's antennae twitched and bobbed as they scented the air. "Why do those soldiers smell so foul?"

Judgment Day

"Feelin' lucky, punk?" Hawthorne antagonized, getting in Anthony's face.

"I'm going to ignore that question," Anthony retorted. It was bad enough that the rest of the hive was whispering about him behind his back. The last thing he needed the horsefly getting on his case. The screams from the medical bay could be heard from yards away. If it hadn't been for Alleo's quick thinking, the Great Hive would have starved for a long time, which would have been a very bad thing for the imminent war.

"*Silence*," Mu-Ra shouted for attention. He was usually calm and calculating, but now he was crouched in a cat-like position, and a hiss wavered from his throat. Somebody watching whispered, "It's her."

The insects packed in front of the main entrance whispered hatefully as Iriana hovered in with a troop of wasp and hornet guards flanking her.

"It's always so *delightful* to see old friends after long periods, wouldn't you agree, Mu-Ra?"

"*Get out*, you witch," Mu-Ra hissed.

"Is that really any way to treat royalty, my mantis friend?" Iriana's guards flicked out their stings. The cry rang out through the Hive.

"Of course not," Iriana said. "I'd very much prefer to be your queen, which I will be soon enough. I've also come to recover my property." She nodded at Anthony, Celia, and Artie. "A good-faith payment to lighten my negotiation terms."

"No," Mu-Ra answered defiantly. "We shall not sacrifice the life of even one insect within the Great Hive's hospitality." He seemed to be speaking more to the gathered insects than to Iriana.

"Sacrifice them!" many of them cried out.

"They have done no wrong."

"*Sacrifice them*!" shouted the crowed, even louder this time.

"Listen to reason, Mu-Ra," Hawthorne pleaded. "They are of no value to us. If Iriana wants them, hand them over. You'll be ridding us of a great deal of dead weight."

"*Learn your place*, Colonel Hawthorne," Mu-Ra hissed. He turned to Iriana. "Begone, oh Queen of Dregs! Your presence is not welcome here or in any other place in this land!"

"Yet *another* decision you shall regret, Mu-Ra," Iriana snarled smugly. She spoke loudly enough for all to hear. "A decision that you *all* shall regret very soon! When my army is marching upon your doorstep, no quarter shall be

given or taken! Your judgment day has come, worms of the 'Great' Hive!" Iriana and her guards withdrew, leaving the hive dwellers with a heightened enmity for Anthony, Celia, and Artie and a seed of fear that would soon blossom into all-consuming warfare.

Stockpiling Anger

"*War*?" the collective cry of Iriana's subjects rang out as the new campaign was decreed. Despite all of Iriana's propaganda, her subjects knew that it would be a war they could hardly afford. After all, the earlier conquests had drained many of their resources, and long periods of foraging would be needed to salvage the amount of supplies necessary for open warfare with such a powerful enemy as the Great Hive. Iriana's impatience for conquest would hardly allow them the required time.

These mutinous complaints reached Iriana the night after she made her fateful visit to the Great Hive. "They have no idea of the enormous stress and pressure this whole affair has brought upon me," Iriana said as she and her private guard indulged on cordial brewed from stolen bee honey.

"Pressure? You're the one who has irresponsibly

brought war upon your people!" a senator from Hive Two pleaded that same night.

"Irresponsible, am I? Well, Senator, I . . ." She paused for a moment before a chilling grin broke out on her face. "Perhaps you're right," she said with a gooey layer of false shame. "Perhaps I am running this kingdom irresponsibly. But it's the unwavering consideration and loyalty of devoted government officials like yourself that a young queen relies on for guidance and assistance. Your reliability shall be rewarded. Guards!" Iriana beckoned the members of her private guard. "Take the nice senator out for a long flight, won't you?"

Snickering understandingly, the guards dragged the away the flailing, kicking senator and flew into the night. That senator was never seen again.

Down in the fungus caverns, which had been flourishing since the recent rain, Iriana sat in elated council with her sister.

"The war on the Great Hive is imminent," she proclaimed with devilish glee. "Those imbeciles don't stand a chance against my army's crushing force. With a little more propaganda, I'll have more than three quarters of the hive armed and battle ready."

"Aren't you worried?"

Iriana almost choked with shock. "Worried about *what*?"

"Those two little ants that exposed your so-called brilliant plans and wiped out almost a whole platoon of your troops. I think they could pose a major threat if they know where you're going to attack next. I certainly hope so."

Vespa's voice carried a note of something Iriana hadn't heard from her in a long time—not rebellion, but hope.

"The hornets are mobilizing!" The Great Hive was in a state of tension as all able-bodied warriors armed themselves for a confrontation with Iriana's army.

"I'm sorry you must dwell in our hive in this state of paranoia and doubt," Mu-Ra apologized in the council room. "We are normally very welcoming of outsiders. Two million is company, but three million is a crowd, you know."

"Why are so many of the hive dwellers antagonizing us?" Celia asked.

"Yeah, like Hawthorne," Anthony muttered under his breath.

"The sad truth is that we of the Great Hive have been living in fear of attack since Iriana became queen of the Hive of Vesthrax. We were expecting these hostilities for months. I suppose you could say we hive dwellers have a history with that hateful hornet.

"We banished and ostracized Iriana after she was convicted of the murder of her own sisters."

"Without a trial?" Celia practically accused.

"Well . . . yes, but the evidence was clear. And she did it with the help of slavemaker ants. Such connections are dangerous and corrupting. She left us no choice."

"*Her own sisters*?" Anthony asked incredulously. It wasn't that Anthony couldn't believe it; he definitely wouldn't put it past Iriana. But to kill *her own kin*? Anthony had a hard time stomaching the thought.

"No doubt she committed countless other cold-blooded murders," Mu-Ra continued.

"Whatever her back story, we need to figure out Iriana's next move," Celia decided. "Would you know something about this, Anthony?"

Anthony shuffled, feeling pressured under the many watchful, piercing eyes of the council. "When I eavesdropped on Iriana, she mentioned something about destroying a viaduct spanning a valley."

"The Clover Valley viaduct!" Guido cried. He unsheathed his saber. "Well, what're we waiting for, huh? Let's strike while the iron's hot!"

"We shall prepare immediately," Mu-Ra decided. "And Anthony shall lead the charge."

"An ant?" Hawthorne let loose a string of oaths. "It's bad enough that he attracted the hornet's attention, but now *he* gets to lead us into yet another suicidal charge?"

"Are you insinuating that you would rather lead this 'suicidal charge'?" Gregorak asked smugly.

"*You're missing the point*!" Hawthorne roared as loudly as possible for a fly. "They'll be the death of us all, and I'm not the only one who knows it. Ask around, Greg, and I'm sure you'll find plenty of others who share my opinions." Hawthorne buzzed away over Anthony and Celia, who were prepared to collapse under the tremendous pressure of being part of the viaduct's defense force.

Anthony stood with his arms straight out as Guido fitted him for his armor. Anthony noticed that his "situation shields," used to convey certain feelings in certain predicaments, each had its own rose with a different color.

"It's the language of flowers, man," Guido explained. "When a yellow rose is on a shield, it means friendship. When you love someone, here it is custom to present him or her with a yellow rose petal." Here Guido winked at Anthony. "The white roses on the main Great Hive gates are for purity, fellowship, innocence, humility, and all that other good stuff. Pink is for sophistication, elegance, and grace. You'll learn more about the language as you get more field experience." By this time Guido was finished fitting Anthony.

"How many ounces does this thing weigh?" Anthony asked as he staggered under the extra weight.

"Plenty." Guido laughed. "Flying insects get the lighter armor with openings in the back. You already have a nice sword, apparently made from human flint steel, forged by dragonflies and decorated with rodent-mined jewels. I gotta hand it to 'im, your dad really had style. But everybody knew that."

"You knew my dad?" Anthony gasped in surprise.

"Almost all of us two million-some-odd hive dwellers knew him. He has his own cairn just before the end of the viaduct facing us."

"Where'd he go?"

"I wish I knew," Guido sighed. "He didn't tell a soul where he was going."

"Hey, Guido."

"Yeah?"

"What's battle like?"

Guido thought for a moment. "I guess ... ugly. That's the only word I can think of."

Battle for the Viaduct

Iriana ordered that her throne room undergo various and thorough renovations. Her throne was raised onto a pyramidal dais of baked clay. The area around the base of the dais was dug into a shallow pit so that the distance Iriana looked down on them from was even greater. To maintain this effect, subjects in the throne room were prohibited from using their wings.

Many of the new tapestries in Iriana's throne room depicted her pre-assumed conquest of the Great Hive. There was a painting of the visible Great Hive dome within a circle, being crossed out by a black rose. She intended this as a perversion of the hive dwellers' language of the flowers. Every soldier in her army was required to have his segment shields (the segmented plates of armor on their abdomens) decorated with a black rose.

It was early in the morning; the sun was just beginning to climb its way up toward the clouds. Iriana was already dressed in full battle regalia, and being the largest insect in the Hive of Vesthrax, she looked quite fierce, even next to the hulking General Razorwing.

"Make sure this is a blow that the Great Hive will not survive. Tell the bombardiers to load the artillery shells with as much shrapnel as they can carry. I want the viaduct to be a pile of rubble at the bottom of the valley, with the rest of the Old Bridge. Go now."

The general nodded and made a cumbersome takeoff, weighed down by his mail-laden wings, and became part of a dark cloud that shifted and buzzed its way toward the valley.

Anthony and Celia rode on Tramonto and Alba to the viaduct, with the tempestuous Colonel Hawthorne and his regiment trailing behind them. You could cut the tension in the air with a knife. Many of the troops jumped at the crack of every pine needle, every swish of trees in the breeze. Even Artie, nestled in a pocket of Tramonto's saddle, was edgy.

Anthony patted him on the head. "This'll be our first real battle," Anthony whispered to him, as if that was something great. But really, Anthony was afraid. He completely related with something Mu-Ra had said before the

regiment departed: "War is one of the greatest flaws of all mortal creatures."

Something else had troubled him and Celia. Before they left, they had heard Hawthorne, Gregorak, and Mu-Ra immersed in a furious argument.

"You shall *not* throw yourself into the front lines, understand?" Mu-Ra had declared. "These are not the times to be settling personal vendettas!"

"This is more my fight than anyone else's," Hawthorne retorted. "I'll do what I must."

"There are close to one million insects in the Great Hive, quite possibly more, that are able-bodied and prepared to give up their lives to defend the freedom of the others in danger of Iriana's persecution," Gregorak said to Hawthorne. "It would be most heinous for them to die in vain because you hastily decide to charge Iriana head on. What satisfaction would one-on-one combat give you?"

"Enough," Hawthorne affronted. "And no insect would die in vain. People have to care for a death to be in vain. And nobody outside of us cares about the death of an insect. To the rest of the world, a dead insect may as well be a speck of dust on the ground." With that, he had buzzed off in a huff.

When Anthony broke from the roiling sea of his thoughts, he realized they were at the start of the viaduct.

The Clover Valley viaduct was 330 feet long, spanning Clover Valley, and was made from the remains of the old human bridge that used to stand there. You could even see small claw marks in the sides of the arches, where the beavers had latched on while helping to flatten the structure.

Hawthorne rotated his wings to signal the troops to a stop.

Across the viaduct, the hornets were waiting.

"Your move, *Colonel*," Hawthorne sneered at Anthony through gritted mandibles.

Anthony refused to be angered by Hawthorne's impudence. If he wanted to be a sour grape, that was his problem. At that moment Anthony needed all the concentration he could get. He invested all of his courage, anger, and determination into one overly theatrical "*Charge*!"

General Razorwing was unimpressed by Anthony's theatricality. He was commanding at the moment around a quarter of the Vesthrax Army, therefore having a more-than-formidable force at his disposal. Due to the continuing conquests, which led to more hives and more larvae, the Vesthrax Army, which numbered well over or close to ten thousand soldiers, was continually growing.

He motioned to his high commanding officers. "No quarter shall be given or taken," he ordered. "Order your factions to fall back after I end the first skirmish." He waved off the officers to the front lines and flew high into the air. He called down to the Great Hive soldiers, "Know that the rubble that lays in the valley after our victory shall be constructed into a monument to the glory of Iriana the Black Rose, Queen of Ten-Thousand Stings and Empress of the New Vesthrax Empire. Unless you surrender now and swear fealty to her Illustrious Majesty, your corpses shall be its mortar!"

"Do your worst, hornet scum!" Gregorak bellowed back,

twirling his axe. The rest of the soldiers rattled their weapons against their rose-decorated shields, sounding like a swarm of the cicadas that lived at the bottom of the valley.

"They have made their choice," General Razorwing said to his troops. "Now, make them regret it."

Crash! The insects leaped into battle like wolves pouncing upon cornered prey. Like most other animal combat, insect fights are notable for ferocity and speed.

Tramonto and Anthony couldn't have been a better matchup. A two-inch hornet had to contend with the weight of the nearly equally sized Tramonto so Anthony could focus on exchanging slashes with the opponent. Tramonto was just as vicious as Nightshade, boxing the hornet's helmet with his front legs and then swinging upward for a roundhouse kick with his hind legs.

That same hornet, plus two wasps, was maimed by Mu-Ra's butterfly kick. Being a master of both Japanese Manti-jitsu and Chinese Manti Fu, he could easily take advantage of his opponents' lack of balance, which would be followed by their lack of limbs … or heads.

Anthony buckled as Tramonto leaped onto the back of a hornet. Before she could aim her sting at Anthony, he hacked off her antennae and plunged his sword into her left eye. *Where are they coming from*? Anthony thought with frustration. Social insects such as hornets or ants prefer chemical pheromone communication for giving orders, and Anthony could smell that General Razorwing was spraying most of his orders into the ground.

Or through *it,* Anthony realized. "Celia!" he cried.

"What?" she called back. "In case you haven't noticed, I'm a little busy over here." Celia had been thrown off of Alba's back and was now fighting beside her. Her sting was locked with a wasp's as they traded blows with their respective blades. The wasp twisted her blade away from Celia's and swung it downward in the style of a guillotine.

Celia somersaulted under the wasp and stung her abdomen before cleaving her apart. She rode over to Anthony.

"I'm ready now," she said, smiling. Celia trailed Anthony to the left side of the viaduct and covered his escape as Tramonto reluctantly crawled underneath all of the action.

It was worse underneath.

The underside of the viaduct was crawling with hornets and wasps shoving explosives in between the wood, stone, and spider webbings that made up the viaduct's foundations. When the others dropped the shrapnel loads, the entire structure would be blown to smithereens. And the shell bearers were already on their way.

"Hawthorne!" Anthony hollered after reaching the top side of the viaduct.

"That's *Colonel* Hawthorne to you, runt!" he snarled back.

"They've set up mines beneath the viaduct. They're going to blow it up!"

"*You* handle it, then," he retorted with unnerving hatred. "I need to complete the frontal assault. I know she's here, and I'm going to find her!"

Suddenly it became apparent to Anthony why Mu-Ra and Gregorak had been so apprehensive about allowing

Hawthorne to participate in the battle: his whole purpose in fighting was to defeat Iriana personally.

And he says I'm *the one playing the hero*, Anthony thought, disgusted at Hawthorne's hypocrisy. He hacked his way over to Celia.

"Hawthorne isn't going to do anything to help," he announced. "I'm taking matters into my own hands."

"And just what"—Celia paused to sting a hornet—"do you suppose we do?"

"Come with me."

"Gee, this sure helps, Anthony," Celia retorted. Underneath the viaduct, Anthony and Celia were surrounded by hornet and wasp engineers attaching explosives. About half of them were moving in for the kill, now that Anthony had dangled himself, Celia, and the two steeds from his spider web rope, interweaved with the web foundation.

Anthony had managed to slide between Tramonto and Alba and had them strapped together in a transparent web harness.

"Hold them off," Anthony ordered Celia. Anthony started unraveling the coils of rope and started spinning and spinning and spinning. Any wasp or hornet that made contact with the spinning, sticky insects became trapped and added to the growing weight. Celia's role was as prey to attract the hornets and wasps to the sticky softball-sized snare.

"And now … we drop." The webbing snapped off from the viaduct, taking the chain of explosives, hornets, wasps, two ants, and their steeds with it.

The Tunnel's Secret

Iriana watched from afar as the shrapnel bearers dropped their shells on the viaduct. At any second the viaduct would explode, taking all of the hive defenders with it.

The shells landed.

Any second…

"You said the cicadas wouldn't interfere!" Iriana berated General Razorwing.

"I can assure you, Your Majesty, that the Clover cicada tribes had nothing to do with this," he pleaded. It was a fearful thing to be at the mercy of Iriana, for she wasn't often inclined to show any.

"They were only seen flying two ants, a grasshopper,

and a cricket to the top of the viaduct before the troops were driven off."

"*Two ants*?" Iriana asked in a dangerously quiet voice. "This level of interference is unacceptable!"

"Do not worry, my lady, it won't continue for long. You see—" The general didn't bother finishing his sentence once he realized that Iriana had stormed off.

Anthony and Celia could hardly comprehend the reality of their great escape or the amount of acclaim they received.

"Congratulations, young ones!" a battle-scarred Gregorak applauded them. "You two fought and thought like true warriors!"

But the cicadas had saved them. One of the tribes had put itself in danger and pulled them—and Tramonto and Alba and Artie—out of the chain of web-coated bombs. Hawthorne, however, had been berated fiercely by Mu-Ra for not taking the initiative to extinguish the bombs.

As the Great Hive celebrated their victory, Anthony strayed from the festivities. He had last seen Artie in Tramonto's saddle. Celia claimed to have seen him bolt for the large tunnel northeast of the main gate. The tunnel entrance was still marked off for further extension, and Artie's scent trailed off a long way down.

For what seemed like an eternity, Anthony staggered blindly through the darkness of the tunnel. Then he heard voices.

"I couldn't care *less* how many of your prize mushrooms were burnt! You have no business here, you old codger!"

"There is surely some misunderstanding. I have some very urgent business with two acquaintances of mine," the voice of an older insect replied.

"Omaha?" Anthony stumbled forward and saw that it was indeed the old dragonfly.

"It's good to see you again, Anthony," Omaha said.

"How did you get down here?"

"I found this long and confusing tunnel when Iriana's raiders forced me from my home."

"Why did they do that?" Anthony asked.

"She wishes to limit unchecked transport throughout her kingdom," Omaha answered. He sighed. "I fear that her increasing paranoia is becoming hazardous to the well-being of the land and its insects."

"This tunnel seems almost suspiciously long," Anthony noticed. He turned to the fat weevil Omaha had been arguing with. "How long does this tunnel stretch?"

"Very long," the weevil answered vaguely, "and still being expanded."

Anthony turned back to Omaha. "You said Iriana was becoming paranoid. About what?"

"Since you two have played a constant role in thwarting her plans, she now has some ridiculous notion that there might be an underground rebellion working against her.

"Come with me," Anthony said. "It sounds like we have a lot to talk about."

Strict orders were given to all Vesthrax Hive subjects that Queen Iriana, in her delicate state of mind, was not to be

disturbed except under the most desperate circumstances. In anticipation of her coming empire, her private guard had been promoted to the imperial guard."

Iriana was desperately producing queen larvae, and the eggs were being laid in comb in her quarters. It was unclear whom she had been mating with, but she was determined to produce as many as possible. "To continue my legacy in the event I am captured or assassinated by the rebellion," Iriana explained.

General Razorwing entered the throne room that evening to report on the progress of a major labor camp established far south of the Rindou Forest.

"Have there been any major difficulties, General?" Iriana asked snappishly.

"Fortunately I have no *major* difficulties to report, Your Majesty," General Razorwing answered, almost nervously, "but—"

"But what?" Iriana bawled. "I will not tolerate any more interference!" Iriana found a thick clay vase and chucked it at the general. "You have allowed the Great Hive to slip through my clutches far too often for my liking!"

Ducking past various other flying ornaments, the general struggled to reassure his raving queen.

"Please, my liege, I was just about to—"

"The rebellion is dogging my efforts constantly, just waiting for the opportunity to end my reign, and you have no assistance to offer except for your pathetic excuses!" Now Iriana was frothing, directing a constant barrage of insults and items at the cowering general.

"I assure you," he said, "that by now my soldiers and

I would have—*ow*—detected even—*ouch*—a whisper of underground—*aagh*—resistance."

"No you wouldn't have because you and your soldiers are useless, incompetent, worthless, despicable maggots!" Iriana threw one last vase before curling up on her throne, breathing heavily.

"The rove beetles can produce a juice that ants simply can't resist," General Razorwing desperately tried to explain to the demented Iriana. "They become so addicted to it that they'll harvest vast crops for just spoonfuls of it!"

Iriana managed to calm herself a bit. "Does the Great Hive know?"

"No."

"See to it that they do." Iriana threw on her favorite traveling cloak. "In fact, let them come freely. When they arrive, I'll have a surprise for them. I'll be overseeing this personally."

"Yourself?"

"Of course. That is, unless you believe I am unfit for the responsibility."

"Nonsense, my queen." The last thing General Razorwing wanted was a second tantrum.

"Very well. Take me to the colony at once." News of his colony being enslaved was more than Anthony could bear. He fell away from reality. He heard Artie howl when Celia and Omaha tried shaking him out of the ball he had curled into. Then Anthony blacked out.

Iriana felt more secure once she learned that three full-grown rats guarded the colony slave camp. It was a stroke of luck, as

mammals and other larger animals almost never offer their services to insects. But the rats were motivated by the promise that the hornets would sting them to death upon refusal.

"Are you sure they can get the job done?" Iriana asked General Razorwing.

"Of course, Your Majesty," General Razorwing assured her. "The ants and their allies have no chance of making it in alive."

"But that's exactly what I want!" Iriana bellowed. Overseers scattered and cowered as Iriana overturned the table they sat at, sending out a spray of shattered glass. She gulped down an entire bottle of wine in three huge swigs, the bottle itself almost meeting General Razorwing's head.

"I don't understand!" he managed to peep out. "Earlier you said the ants made a valuable workforce."

Iriana was now in hysterics. "This isn't about what I said then. It's about what I want *now*!" Iriana quickly found another bottle of wine and downed it. She slumped onto her chair overlooking much of the mining done by the ant slaves.

"I'm such a wreck," Iriana moaned. "It's all my sister's fault. It's all *their* fault," she wailed, pointing at nothing.

General Razorwing immediately knew Iriana was referring to both her crippled, incarcerated sister and her long-dead ones. They had always teased Iriana mercilessly. When her elders spoke of Iriana's frailty, they meant mental frailty, not physical weakness.

"If it makes you feel any better, Your Grace, the hive defenders have arrived."

"Really?" Iriana's face seemed to light up. "In that case, send the army to the Great Hive."

"What?"

"Don't ask questions, General. Just do it! The Great Hive will be distracted, giving me the perfect opportunity to strike them from two directions."

"Two directions, Your Majesty?" General Razorwing couldn't stand it any longer. Your reasoning makes no sense! What exactly do you want to do? Kill the ant or attack the Great Hive?"

"Both. Simultaneously."

"Please explain."

"The ant and the Hive soldiers accompanying him will be kept busy at the slave colony, giving *us* time to launch an attack."

"In plain sight?"

"Of course not."

The general was bewildered.

"Oh yes, didn't I tell you?" Iriana asked. "My men are now making their way down a recently finished tunnel leading directly into the Great Hive."

Anthony couldn't recall how he had gotten to his home colony or why the Great Hive sent so many soldiers with him. He said nothing on the entire trip there. His mind was fully consumed by his anger at Iriana. Celia, on the other hand, had been content to stay at the Great Hive in case of an emergency.

Anthony was drowning in a flood of machine-like

devotion for his home colony that is hardwired into the brain of every ant. How could he have denied it? Why had he not felt this burning guilt but a day after leaving his colony? Why hadn't Celia? There were so many questions but no time to find the answers.

I should be fighting with the others aboveground, Anthony thought, *but I must find my mom. I never should have left her alone.*

It hadn't occurred to Anthony that he had been the first to make it inside, and that was the reason why no guards had found him yet. In his haze he hadn't noticed that his allies were occupying Iriana's forces. Confused and frustrated, Anthony slumped against the dirt wall.

How did I get in here? he wondered. *Did I sneak in? Yes, yes, that's what happened. That dead wasp fell on me by the entrance. I fell in through one of the vertical tunnels.*

"Looking for your mommy, little Anthony?" a voice taunted him. Anthony turned around to find Iriana slouched against the tunnel wall behind him. He lunged at her in a blind rage, but she easily sidestepped his attack. Was she getting faster? Or was Anthony just getting slower?

"You should have stayed with your friends aboveground," Iriana said. "At least the rats will tear them apart quickly. You won't enjoy such a luxury." Iriana flew down another vertical tunnel, and Anthony darted after her. He found her perched on the other side of a mammoth chamber filled with ants.

Anthony recognized the chemical scents of many of them, but none behaved as normal. They all shared the same glazed expression, grinding their mandibles as they worked constantly and strenuously to harvest the crops growing from the floor of the chamber.

"Do you recognize any old friends?" Iriana laughed down to him. "They probably don't recognize *you.* They work for hours a day with their only pay being a squirt of rove beetle juice." Anthony seethed at the hornet's words. An ant's sight is relatively poor, but he didn't need eyes to see the oppression and stress these brainwashed ants had been through.

He didn't quite understand how brainwashed they were till he saw his mother... and she turned away.

This put Anthony over the edge. He had found his mother in tough conditions, among thousands of brainwashed ants, and she didn't recognize him.

"*Mother*!" Anthony cried as he rushed the beetles in the center of the room. Every guard that tried to stop him was butchered, and when he reached the beetles, he knew no mercy. He flung the juice-dripping carcasses to the other end of the room, where the rest of the wasps and hornets were amassing to destroy him. Before they could shake themselves free of the dead beetles, the ants were on them in a flash, killing and maiming anything standing between them and the sweet juice of the rove beetles.

Anthony was dragged, kicking and squealing, out of his colony. In his blind rage, he didn't see who it was; it might have been Gregorak. He did remember biting him furiously. The raid had been a massacre; the armored rats had devastated three-quarters of the attack force. When the Hive warriors reached the concentration room, they found the damage Anthony had wreaked upon the Vesthraxians. Many of the remaining wasps and hornets

retreated but not very far. It was clear that while the Great Hive had successfully infiltrated the colony, completely freeing it from Iriana's control would yet be an issue.

Anthony didn't rest easily that night, as he rolled two ideas around in his mind for hours: First, he would like nothing more than to rip Iriana's smug, laughing head off of her shoulders, and second, he knew why Hawthorne did what he did at the viaduct.

Hawthorne's Soliloquy

General Razorwing was worried; Iriana hadn't left her room since returning to the hive and depositing a few eggs. It was still dark outside, and Iriana had been shrieking and moaning with pain for hours, although once he thought he had heard a contented chuckle. When his queen's cacophony ceased for a few moments, General Razorwing decided to investigate.

Upon entering, he saw that Iriana's room had been wrecked. Nothing was lit inside the room, save for the flickering light of his lantern.

"Put out that light, General!" Iriana's voice barked from the darkness. General Razorwing immediately did so and closed the door behind him.

"Are you all right, my queen?" he asked. "I heard you screaming earlier."

"Actually, I've never felt better. A potion I drank last evening just had some painful side effects."

"Potion?"

"That's right," Iriana answered. "Have I ever told you that Amazonian blood runs in my veins, General? I did a bit of research on my family tree, and once I found that I had exotic, powerful traits lying dormant inside of me, I decided to expose them."

"D-did you experiment with this earlier?"

"Yes. Three weeks ago. I tried an experimental version of the potion; it turned my wings red for two days. I pretended to be bedridden with fever to conceal them."

General Razorwing gulped nervously; none of this sounded very good to him.

"Now that I have tried the perfected serum, and it has taken its effect, I realize that our army has an unstoppable new secret weapon."

"What weapon would that be?" General Razorwing asked anxiously.

"Me." Iriana finally gave the general permission to relight his lantern.

Overnight, Iriana had undergone an evil transformation. Her deep-rooted Amazonian traits had indeed fully exposed themselves; in a few hours she had grown to three inches in length. Her exoskeleton now showed an iridescent purplish hue, while her normally transparent wings were a sickly orange. Worst of all, her stinger was no longer paralyzing—it was deadly.

General Razorwing was stunned with fear and awe. "Your Majesty," he managed to wheeze out, "you've … changed."

"For the better, General," she said with a grin. As she lowered her head to General Razorwing's level, he noticed that her compound eyes had darkened to an evil green. "As you can see, no insect will be able to stand up to me. I even believe that the serum may lengthen my lifespan by *years*! And even if I should die, I have a backup plan."

Iriana nudged a large, dark egg before the general. "A larvae that shall inherit my new natural power! I trust you know where to hide it." The diabolical glint in her eyes told General Razorwing that should he make a mistake, she would kill him without the slightest consideration.

The enormous hornet queen curled up in slumber.

"General?"

"Yes, Your Majesty?"

"When you leave, bring me back some food. I'm starving." "I'll see what vegetation is left in storage."

"No vegetables."

"*Pardon*?"

General Razorwing was confused and disturbed by her request. Wasps and hornets had a strictly vegetarian diet.

Iriana grinned at the large hornet that she now dwarfed. "Right now, what I need is some bloody, fresh meat."

In the Great Hive, Anthony awoke from a troubled rest to an optimistic, cheerful sight. Despite the worried atmosphere, the Great Hive denizens still had decorated for the Moon Festival, which began that day. The balconies,

stairwells, and corridors were resplendent in moonstones. And between the grand spiral staircase and the main gate stood Celia's old sculpture of Agoz, imposing and decked out with layers of gold and silver.

"Do you like it?" a voice asked from beside Anthony. He turned around to find Celia standing next to him. "I'm head of the decoration committee. I showed them my designs, and they liked them. Go figure."

Anthony cracked a smile; his friend always knew just how to cheer him up. But then he asked the question that had been nagging him all of the previous night: "Why didn't you go back."

Celia gave a sad smile. "The only friend I ever knew there almost got himself killed yesterday. At least you had something, someone to go back to." She threw one arm around Anthony's shoulders. "I know what went on yesterday. Don't blame yourself. If anything, we should both be blaming Iriana for turning our adventure into a living nightmare."

Anthony smiled at Celia. After a larvaehood of arguing, they finally had something they could completely and truly agree on: their hatred for Iriana and their love for the Great Hive and all of their friends there.

"Thanks, Celia," Anthony said, "but I think there's someone else who needs comforting more than I do."

When Anthony reached Hawthorne's room, Gregorak and Alleo were already waiting there.

"He's been in his room sulking for hours," the goliath beetle sighed.

"Are you sure you want to go in?" Alleo asked. Anthony was.

Hawthorne was clutching a watercolor painting when Anthony walked in. It was of a beautiful hornet, slim and graceful, lacking all of the cruel features that denoted Iriana.

"Did you know her?" Anthony asked. Hawthorne snapped out of his reverie, his forest-green compound eyes rimmed red with inner pain.

"We were lovers," Hawthorne answered softly. Though this startled Anthony, it was clear that the two had had a strong relationship.

"What was her name?" Anthony asked.

"Vespa. She was a princess, heir to the Vesthraxian throne. Iriana's sister. I had just reached the Great Hive; I was only a few years old, adolescence for a horsefly. We met in Rindou, in the branches of a maple tree. She was so beautiful, so wonderful, and we were both very young. It was a match made in heaven. We could never have offspring, true, but we were naïve. Our love seemed enough.

"We met as often as we could in that tree. It wasn't that we were forbidden to meet, but that our lives kept us apart too often. We met in the maple tree for almost three years, until we planned to marry. We were an odd couple, as you might imagine. We tried to keep our love a secret, but many found out. Vespa suffered the worst. People that had once respected and loved her spat at and slandered her. But then her sister came along."

"What did Iriana do to you?" Anthony whispered sympathetically. She had taken something precious away from the both of them.

"It wasn't what she did to *me*," Hawthorne explained hoarsely, "it was what she did to Vespa. You see, Iriana was jealous of her sister's love. It had always eluded her, yet Vespa found it and the comfort it brought. So she took Vespa from me."

"She just took her away?"

"Yes. All at once, Vespa just stopped coming to our meeting place. Iriana even left a note that read, *'Vespa has gone away, to a place you can never find her. Perhaps you shall meet again someday: in death.'* I know that Iriana killed her." Hawthorne wept. "Just like she killed all of her other sisters and her mother. Or if she isn't dead, she was imprisoned in some dungeon to curl up and rot. Not knowing is the worst pain of all."

"When Iriana is defeated, you and I can find out the truth," Anthony promised. Hawthorne didn't answer but instead fell back into his reverie.

When Anthony left to recover, he found the hive in a buzz of activity.

"Greg!" he called as the beetle flew past. "What's going on?"

"Treachery, young ant!" the warrior beetle shouted. "The Great Hive has been breached!"

Anthony and Celia sat on Tramonto and Alba, Alleo buzzed with fury, and Guido twirled his rapier in agitation as soldiers dragged away Iggy, the hysterical weevil.

"You'll never win now, fools!" he screamed. "You're too late, too late!" From a long way down the tunnel, the buzz of digger wasps and sand wasps could be heard. The taller insects stood on top of each other to form a wall, blocking the invaders off from the Great Hive.

"Get ready!" Gregorak called to the other soldiers. Anthony watched from behind as the insect wall buckled with the force of the first charge. The wall proved to be an impressive technique; the few wasps that squeezed through were decapitated before they could pass. Moments later the wasps retreated, leaving the hive defenders to catch their breath.

"They are sure to return in time," Mu-Ra predicted. "And our intelligence has informed us that the Vesthraxian Army is coming to destroy the Great Hive. If we cannot meet them halfway, they will arrive and do irreparable damage to the Great Hive." He turned to Gregorak. "Take as many students as you can to the lower levels and position armed guards at the tunnel entrance." Mu-Ra turned to Guido. "Rally every insect, arachnid, and crustacean that can carry a weapon. We may outnumber Iriana's army, but in strength, we are too evenly matched."

"Come with me to the armory," said Angela, the Jamaican pill bug from the council meeting. Alleo, Anthony, and Celia followed her closely as she led them to the warfare department of the Great Hive armory. Among the items being carried and rolled out to the main gate were barrels of flammable oil, catapults, ballistae, and chunks of quartz.

They found Tramonto, Alba, and other steeds were being suited with protective mesh and plates. Most fearsome were the war locusts, hissing and rearing, wearing horned helmets for goring opponents. Celia's armor ended in a flowing mesh gown.

"Is the gown really necessary, ma'am?" Celia asked.

"No," the pill bug answered, "but it helps to distinguish the males from the female insects on the battlefield."

"Is that really a necessity?"

"Well, no, but… I'll reconsider that later. Just keep it on for now."

At his own request, Alleo's shield had been adorned with the insignia of his hive on Zephyr's Knoll: a mulberry within a cloud. It was a proud yet sad reminder of the home that Iriana and her vicious general had taken away from him.

"All warriors and trained apprentices, report to the main gate for departure!" Guido's voice could be heard calling from the grand spiral staircase all the way down to the lowest levels of the Great Hive.

"Are you ready for battle, young ant?" a voice asked Anthony. He turned to see Hawthorne riding astride Nightshade and for once, wearing a beaming smile on his face.

Iriana was about to catch up with her army right after she finished tucking into two whole locusts.

They still hadn't been enough.

"Your Majesty!" General Razorwing called. "It's time we caught up with the army. My sources have confirmed that the Great Hive intends to meet us halfway."

"Excellent," she hissed. "I do believe I've restrained my predatory instincts long enough." Laughing maniacally, Iriana flew off to join her army, twice as fast as any normal hornet could fly.

Death and Rain

The Great Hive's warriors flew with all haste as teams of locusts carried mobile and stationary weapons through the air. Anthony's, Celia's, and Alleo's senses were overtaken by the buzz of anticipation for the battle to come. It was most depressing for the hive defenders that they were flying into battle on the first day of the Moon Festival. Anthony thought of little Artie left behind with the guards trying to keep the wasps at bay in the tunnel.

Below them was Magnolia Glade, a midsized circular clearing that marked the point directly in between the Great Hive and the Vesthrax Hive. Here they landed; in the distance, the Vesthraxian Army could be heard singing a death chant.

At the opposite side of the glade, Iriana's army landed.

General Razorwing and his soldiers made way for the newly transformed hornet queen.

The morale held by the Great Hive's warriors took a steep plunge when Iriana stepped onto the battlefield. Anthony saw through a spyglass Iriana's transformation and how many of his fellow soldiers cowered at the sight of her.

"Normally I would ask you all if you wished to surrender," Iriana called smugly, "but I can see that you all have placed yourselves far beyond help."

"Today, Iriana," Mu-Ra answered, "your reign *ends*!

Iriana looked down at General Razorwing. "It's time, old ally. But before we attack, just one thing."

"Yes, Your Majesty?"

"I get first kill!" Iriana lunged forward, and the battle began.

The beautiful Magnolia Glade was becoming a graveyard of blood, gore, and dying insects. The Great Hive's vanguard was consumed by fiery coals from hornet catapults. Anthony and Alleo were among the hive defenders to meet the enemy in the air, crashing head-on into wasps and hornets that were bearing down on them. Alleo's sting disemboweled the wasp that had been trying to tear out his heart; Anthony decapitated a hornet as Tramonto kicked it in mid-jump.

Celia and Alba were on the ground and were besieged by wasps with long pikes. One jabbed through Alba's eye, sending the cricket into a rage. Oblivious to the pointed weapons impaling her, she trampled and ran down any enemy in her way.

Alleo had found General Razorwing, the hornet who had destroyed his home. The general tore at him from all sides with his blade-covered wings, sending up a spray of hair and flesh every time Alleo attacked. The general's war hammer crashed against Alleo's locked shield and sword, crushing them both. In a rage, Alleo threw himself at General Razorwing, his sting seeking the general's chest. Before he could deal the final blow, however, Alleo felt himself being lifted off of the ground by a powerful grip.

"I wonder," said Iriana, practically crushing Alleo in her grip, "if you bees taste as sweet as your honey."

"Well, you won't find out today!" Hawthorne cried as Nightshade pounced on Iriana's back. The ferocious cave cricket tore at and bit the hornet queen's wings before being flipped onto the ground.

Iriana was surrounded by Alleo, Anthony, Celia, Hawthorne, Mu-Ra, Guido, and Gregorak.

"Your time has come, witch!" roared Gregorak.

"I was going to make your deaths quick," said Iriana. "But now I think I'm going to kill all of you *very slowly*."

Any other insects that interfered were destroyed by Iriana. Even Gregorak was tossed carelessly into the air. Iriana was increasingly frustrated by her inability to kill Mu-Ra. What the old mantis lacked in strength, he compensated for with speed and agility.

"I'm growing bored with this game," Iriana sighed. She whistled for more of her troops, and they launched themselves in front of her. Through the wall of hornets and

wasps Anthony saw Hawthorne follow Iriana to the high, rocky part of the glade.

"Celia," he cried, "come with me!" Anthony prayed that they would reach Iriana first, in case Hawthorne decided to do something he might regret.

As they cleared the penultimate rock, a hornet came up on Anthony by surprise. Before he could react, the hornet had stung Tramonto in the abdomen.

Anthony and Tramonto crashed headlong into the ground.

"Tramonto!" Celia stopped next to Anthony to examine the damage.

"You go after Iriana," Celia ordered Anthony. "I'll guard Tramonto until the medics can get to him." She paused to clash her sword against the sting of a wasp.

"Go!" Anthony climbed up the rock face, ducking past flying minerals, coals, and shattering quartz clusters. When he reached the top of the rock, he happened upon a terrifying scene.

From there he could see the teeming masses of armed insects destroying each other. Explosions and small fires tore apart the battleground while warriors trampled over fallen allies and enemies in order to reach an opponent. Stings tore flesh, swords rattled against shields, and fire consumed all.

In front of Anthony were Iriana and Hawthorne. Nightshade lay injured on the ground, screaming for Hawthorne. Hawthorne stood resiliently before Iriana, although he was practically choking on his own blood. A recent wound ran with red-yellow liquid where some of Iriana's venom had dripped in and was beginning to take effect.

"Anthony," he wheezed out, "run. Join your friends in battle. I'll be fine."

"Sir," Anthony said, "I can't leave you here."

"Feel free to join him, little ant," Iriana sneered. "I don't think one dead ant will make a difference to anybody."

"I don't think a dead hornet would warrant many tears either," Anthony retorted smugly.

"Tell that to your mentor here," Iriana corrected. "There's an anemic hornet in a dark dungeon that got quite a few tears from this old soldier. Isn't that right, Hawthorne? She'll be dead soon, anyway, so why don't you join her?"

Nightshade lost it. The screaming cricket charged into Iriana, almost throwing her off of the rock. While Iriana grappled at the rocky edge with Hawthorne's steed, Anthony tried to escort Hawthorne to safety. On the way down, they were blinded by smoke from a coal that had ignited dry brush.

"Leave me, Anthony," Hawthorne told him. "I'm beyond help. I know Vespa's alive, and that's all I wished to know. Make sure she knows I still love her, even in death."

"I will, sir," Anthony said.

"I was wrong about you," Hawthorne admitted. "You'll make a great hive champion. Stay true to the Hive and make sure that Iriana doesn't get her filthy claws on it." Hawthorne gasped for breath as his airways constricted.

"See you on the other side, boy." Anthony held Hawthorne in his arms, silently mourning for a noble creature who was now lost.

"Where is Iriana?" Anthony demanded to know from Gregorak, whose troops held their position next to a ballista.

"She and her imperial guard are retreating to the Vesthrax Hive," the weary but resilient goliath beetle answered. His axe cut down yet another hornet and another and another. "Celia and I will make sure Hawthorne's body is safe," he promised.

"Good, because I'm going after Iriana," Anthony said.

"Are you mad? You can't possibly catch up with her at this rate. And besides, you are no match for that monster."

"Hawthorne's dying wish was that we keep Iriana from the Great Hive. She won't rest until she has it, so we have no choice but to kill her. Tell Celia she's been the best friend any ant could ask for. And please take care of Artie." Anthony tore off his body armor, lessening the splitting pain in his exoskeleton. The pain, however, turned out to be a blessing when Anthony saw that he now sported a pair of strong, transparent wings.

Anthony had never before felt so free and yet so doomed at the same time. He was finally flying, and yet he was most likely flying to a painful, agonizing death. Just ahead, Anthony could see Iriana flying with her imperial guard.

Iriana smelled Anthony from a far distance. "Exterminate that pest," she ordered her guards. "I've got a sick sister to visit."

Anthony saw the guards perform an aerial u-turn and

press in on him from both sides, holding their halberds beneath them.

"Are you ready for this?" he asked them.

Celia and Alleo had heard from Gregorak that Anthony had left to fight Iriana. Darks clouds rolled in, and the ground shook with thunder. Raindrops began pelting the battleground, creating a grisly slush of gore and mud.

In the center of the battlefield General Razorwing stood, crushing those who dared to oppose him with his war hammer and shredding them with his wings.

Celia turned to Alleo with a grim smile on her face. "For Anthony," she said.

"For Anthony!" Alleo agreed. Celia wrenched a long spear from the grasp of a yellowjacket missing half of its body. The two of them charged the general, who accepted their challenge with enthusiasm.

"Come get splattered, you maggots. When I'm done with the two of you, you'll—" General Razorwing didn't have time to finish his sentence because Celia had just speared his left compound eye, clouding his multifaceted vision with blood.

"You cowardly scum!" he roared in anguish. "Come fight me face to face!" Alleo did indeed fight General Razorwing face to face, scarring the general to the point where there was hardly a face to be seen. Alleo left General Razorwing on the ground, screaming in agony as a legion of bees bearing the standard of the Zephyr Knoll's hive exacted their revenge upon the insect that burned down their home.

Iriana slithered through the slowly deluging fungus caverns. This was where rainwater would collect in an overflowing amount to nourish the tree that hosted the Hive of Vesthrax. She couldn't wait to tell Vespa about her lover's death. It would be the perfect way to end her life—in anguish, just as she had always been forced to live.

Iriana stopped; she caught an all-too-familiar scent.

"Anthony?" she asked, already knowing the answer. She looked down at the battle-scarred young ant. "So, you survived my guards."

"Honestly, why did you hire such idiots to be your imperial guards? Perhaps it reflects on your own way of thinking," Anthony mocked her. "Are you going to stand and fight? Or will I have to chase you down?" By the time he was finished asking the question, Iriana had fled into the darkness of the caverns.

Anthony dashed in on all six limbs. The rainfall had strengthened to a downpour. and the fungus caverns were being swept by a torrent of rushing, unstoppable water. Without any light or guidance, Anthony found himself plunging down a Niagara of rainwater.

"I can smell you, Anthony," Iriana's gloating voice echoed through the flooding darkness. "You really *are* a stupid little bug to have followed me here and to have meddled in *my* business. To have turned a simple purchasing of land into a full-fledged war."

"You *wanted* this war!"

"I wanted revenge! *There's a difference*!" On instinct,

Anthony threw himself to the left; Iriana's sting passed a hair's breadth from his head.

Anthony felt his way past the fibrous roots of the enormous tree till he found a muddy bank. Iriana found him. The two of them fought, sword against sword, sting against bite. To Anthony's advantage, Iriana used the same slim sword that she always had. The two of them spun, parried, and jabbed, matching each other blow for blow in an erratic dance of death.

A kick from Iriana sent Anthony soaring two feet into the air and into the swirling water. The rainwater gushed from countless seams and gaps in the high cavern ceilings. Between the columns of falling water, Anthony could just make out Iriana's orange wings cutting through the darkness like twin shark fins.

Anthony blocked her sword jabbing out from the roiling depths and found soggy but still solid land.

"Who's the one running now, ant?" Iriana sneered. It was true; Anthony was being forced back, hiding behind water pillars. Through these Iriana lunged after Anthony, her gaping jaws illuminated by forks of lightning splintering the dark sky.

Turn for turn and twist for twist, Anthony and Iriana dogged each other off a slippery slope of moss, down which the water tore. Anthony managed to grab hold of a mushroom jutting from the wall; Iriana climbed after him.

"I know these caverns too well for you to escape," she gloated. A swipe from Iriana knocked Anthony back into the water. This time the current carried him away from Iriana. Underneath a small waterfall, Anthony saw what

looked like an underwater cave, hidden by a trapdoor; if it could give him time to recover, it was worth the risk.

When Anthony swam through the trapdoor, he saw what looked like Iriana preparing to attack him. But it wasn't.

Princess Vespa the Second was surprised and relieved that the young ant had come and not Iriana. Her cell was almost full; it wasn't long before the two of them would drown.

"Are you Vespa?" Anthony asked.

"Yes, young ant," she answered with the voice of an angel. "How did you know?"

"Hawthorne's dying wish was that you knew he still loved you and hadn't forgotten you."

Vespa's gaze turned steely. "The ground should be mud by now. Loosen the bars to my cell." Anthony obliged, ducking under the water and leaning into the muck to slide out the bars.

"Get onto my back," she ordered Anthony. "We're going to pay my sister a visit."

Vespa dove like a hawk upon seeing Iriana. She didn't seem to feel any fear, Anthony noticed, despite the obvious change in her sister's appearance.

"*Impossible*!" Iriana roared when she saw Vespa. She effortlessly knocked her from the air. "I'll destroy you for this, ant," she roared after Anthony. Vespa launched herself out of the water and onto Iriana. The two sisters grappled ferociously. Infuriated and wanting to kill Anthony first, Iriana bit off one of her sister's legs.

Anthony was just beginning to climb the wall of the

cavern, pressed against it to avoid the downpour of rainwater, when Iriana pounced on him, just as he had planned it.

After he had slathered himself in his bottled spider oil that Omaha had given him, Anthony jumped into Iriana's mouth. While Iriana gagged on the taste of Anthony's spider oil, he jumped out. When Iriana had come to her senses, Anthony's spider web rope had tied her to the root she stood on.

Iriana noticed, panicking, that the water level was quickly climbing up to her. "You haven't won yet, Anthony!" Iriana roared. With that, she swung her sword down at Anthony, maiming him and sending him tumbling into the water.

Iriana laughed with an insane glee, until she saw Vespa flying toward the ceiling with Anthony in tow.

"*No*! I am queen of all!" Iriana frothed. "I cannot be thwarted so easily!" The water was sweeping over her now.

Vespa and Anthony alighted on solid ground just four inches above Iriana. Vespa was holding Iriana's crown.

"She has poisoned the old queenhood," she declared. "There must be no trace left." Vespa dropped the crown into the roiling water.

"You fool! Damn you!" Iriana screamed dementedly. The crown bobbed temptingly close. The water was climbing above her head.

Vespa and Anthony left Iriana to her fate.

As the water clouded her vision and swam into her airways, Iriana saw the crown, still floating, just out of reach. Although the memories would stain the foundations of the Hive of Vesthrax for generations to come, Iriana the Terrible was swept away under a torrent of swirling, crushing water, still reaching and howling for her crown and her queenship.

Epilogue

Mu-Ra and Vespa immediately negotiated the release of the land that Iriana had colonized. All Vesthraxian occupational forces fell back, and reconstruction of the Vesthraxian kingdom began.

"Our holy land has been desecrated, yes, but I will do what I can to heal it," Vespa declared. And as she believed Hawthorne would have wished, she had him buried under the maple tree in which they used to meet.

Back at the Great Hive, the wasp invasion had been quelled and the tunnel destroyed. The Moon Festival kicked off wonderfully. There was music, dancing, wonderful food, and no worry of violence.

Celia and Alleo found Anthony just before the grand unveiling of a new work of art Celia had finished.

"I've made it especially for this occasion," Celia explained to Anthony, beaming. "In light of recent events."

Every insect in the Great Hive looked down from balconies or up from them as Mu-Ra and Celia unveiled the artwork.

"This statue is a monument to an insect that has taught us all that even in the face of unspeakable evil, no matter how small or great, one act of courage can bring back the light," Mu-Ra announced happily.

"I now present to you all," Celia announced, "Anthony, the Great Hive's Champion of Courage!"

Anthony's heart leaped with pride as Celia revealed the statue and everyone in the Great Hive cheered.

It was a life-size statue of Anthony, his father's sword held high in triumph.

At the base of the statue an engraved golden plaque read, "Anthony Daemond:

A Real Hero."